Extraordinary Deviations

Transgender Erotica

I0570476

Raven Kaldera

Gressive Press
Cambridge, MA

ISBN 978-1-61390-086-4

First paperback edition December 2013

Published by Gressive Press
an imprint of Circlet Press, Inc.
39 Hurlbut Street
Cambridge, MA 02138
www.circlet.com

Contents

Only Fate

Fucking women. That's the only thing that kept running through my mind when she said it. "It's your fate. I can read it right here. You're doomed to do this thing. You can't escape Fate."

"Why the fuck not?" I asked. My hands gripped the edge of the table and her lamp with its fringed shade teetered a little, cast fluttering shadows over the spread of her cards, flickered on her face below that stupid turban she wore in order to look all mysterious and Miss Cleo-like. "Why can't I just choose?"

"Well, some things you can choose," she said. "But not this. Look, I'm just telling you what I see. You have to let go of this relationship, and you have to go east again and pick up the work you put down. If you don't do it, everything will go wrong for you— like it has been, like you said. And you'll end up doing it anyway because Fate will just push you over there eventually anyway."

"Are you telling me it's some sort of punishment?" I grunted out angrily. *Fucking women. All my life, it's been women telling me what to do. Fuck them.*

She opens her mouth, as if she's about to say something smug, and then suddenly stops. "I don't know," she admits. Well, thank some Bitch up there for some honesty, finally. "You believe in the Gods, you told me," she says. "Why don't you ask the Fates? The three women? Maybe they'll tell you."

"That's all I need. More fucking women telling me what to do." Oops. That wasn't supposed to come out of my mouth. She sat back, her eyes widening, emotions fighting it out on her face. Before one of them could win, I sighed and pulled out my wallet-chip. "Never mind. Thank you for trying. I'll show myself out." I punched in thirty, passed the chip over her credit-wand and left. Why didn't I find a male diviner? Because of the four that I emailed from my chip, none had open appointments for the next three weeks. Even Astreyson was traveling to the MariCorp islands for a convention. Only these damn bitches left, damn it, with their smug superiority and their too-much-eyeliner pics on the diviner's union page.

I jabbed at my chip as I sat on the lightrail on my way home, scrubbed my finger along the glowing lines—it only took me a couple of seconds to find my email—and watched the page unfold in large-scale in front of my eyes. It was translucent; I could see through it to the facing row of people, many of whom were also holding their chips and staring off into space. The hologram was keyed to my retina, just like theirs, so we couldn't see each other's pages, although I could see some of them moving their lips, dictating subvocalized letters. I deleted all the spam with quick eye movements. I didn't want to see any omens in them. Yes, I believe in Gods. A few times in my life, they've actually spoken to me. And omens? I don't listen when those songs appear on my chip that I didn't download, that describe my problem in ways that piss me off. I erase them, OK? Go away. It's not your era any more. Go back to the ancient times where you belong and leave me alone.

There were ads along the side of the hologram. One was for Club Fatima. Dammit.

I switched to a different page with a jerk of my eyelids so hard that I almost closed the whole window. The ad that slapped at the side of my vision is for Jim Weaver, Attorney at Law. I switched again. This time it was another club, Spin City. I turned off the chip. No more. I'll just stare at the white walls of the lightrail all the rest of the way home. I remember when those walls had posters and things, but now they're white, because the majority of people on the lightrail use this time to check their chips and a white wall is so much less distracting when you're staring at a hologram. Of course that meant fifteen minutes of boredom for me, but... The lightrail swoomed to a halt and the door opened. "Please evacuate the train. We are having technical difficulties. You will receive free passes upstairs."

I grumbled my way out with the rest of the grumbling crowd, kloms away from my home stop, and got my free pass. Not that this would make up for the helicab I would have to pay for, or the hour I would to have to wait before enough helicabs showed up to take this whole crowd. Bah. On the street, the cold and slightly salty air hit my face, even though we were kloms from the water. Somehow the artificial corporate islands all smelled like seawater, no matter where you were. I squinted across the street in hopes of finding a barstool I could curl up on and wait, and yellow letters curled across my vision, juxtaposed on a spiral. SPIN CITY.

∽

Sometimes you just have to face things down. I went in, suspiciously. People were dancing under glitter-filled lights. I hated the popular effect of light-particle glitter sifting down through the spotlights, it made me feel like there were bugs flying around my head and I wanted to swat them. A woman smiled at me, her full lips painted and parted. I pulled my collar up and didn't make eye contact. *No more women. Ever. I'm tired of being hurt by them, tired of being controlled by them. Come on, Bitches, I'm here, what am I supposed to see?*

A body caught my eye, dancing, and I had to stop and look because it looked so much like Kevin, the guy I was breaking up with. Oh, not so much like him that I thought he might actually be here, dancing in a club—the figure had black hair, not Kevin's medium brown, and anyway Kevin didn't dance in clubs. Kevin was soft-spoken and wore old-fashioned glasses and spent all his time researching things that grew on the bottom of the ocean. Kevin would never hurt me deliberately, he cried when he told me that this job was his dream job, his once-in-a-lifetime opportunity, and he was so sorry, he knew I couldn't come along because of my security clearance, he was so sorry...

I dragged my thoughts away from that. The figure was lean, hard-bodied, tight pants over lean muscled legs with a modest bulge at the crotch, and a sleeveless shirt that seemed to be made of a hundred strands of whipping yarn. It showed nice deltoid definition, though. Long, long black hair, and I couldn't see the face, but who cared. Screw the omens. I wanted to dance with this one.

He smiled at me as I approached and moved invitingly closer with a few hip-thrusts. His face was large-lipped, pointed-chinned, androgynous. A hint of beard shadow. It didn't take long before my hands were on his hips, my pelvis against his, and then... My hands moved up through the shaking blue fringe of his shirt and found small breasts, and I was so surprised that I moved away from him for a moment. "What the hell—" I began.

"What's the matter?" he said. Deep, smooth baritone voice. He grinned at me and dragged the threads of his shirt aside for a moment, exposing a small and perfect teat. "You need your men manly and your women womanly? Come on, I know you're bisexual."

"How the hell do you know anything about—" I began again, but he took my hands and put them on his tits, pulled my hips closer again, and shifted me into the rhythm. His eyes were dark, heavy-lidded, and he looked startlingly like a girl for a moment, a heavy-featured, sultry girl. His hands found my ass, and I realized that I was hard. "Are you on the way to male, or female?" I asked, hoping he could hear me over the music. I was trying to be cool, to figure out which he was, how he wanted to be treated.

"I'm not on the way to anything except you," he said, and then he moved closer and kissed me. I could feel stubble, and a mouth that devoured me and bit my tongue gently. The small breasts pressed against me, and the hard arms gripped me with surprising strength. Just when I was getting my bearings—all right, I'm no prude, but this was moving a bit fast—he abruptly back up, seized my hand, and pulled me out of the flickering light-bugs and into the darkness of the back of the club. Those narrow hips swung like a woman's, sashaying ahead of me, and I almost switched mental pronouns—no. I wasn't even going to think about whether this person counted as male or female, nor what that made me, made my promises to myself. I hoped that he wasn't going to take us into a bathroom—some places had gender-neutral bathrooms, or the set of three in a row, but older places often still didn't, at least on this island. I didn't want to know which one he'd pick if there were only two.

Instead, he found a darkened back corridor and pressed me up against the wall, soft breasts over hard pecs and lats. He undid his pants and then mine, and held two hard cocks in his hand together, stroking both of them. I gasped and writhed against the wall, against him, and then took over stroking both of them as his hands went all over me, down my ass till his fingers wormed their way into my crack. My thumb ran down his cock to the bottom ... and found, instead of furred or even naked balls, that it vanished into warm wetness.

My eyes must have shown what I felt, but he just chuckled at me and took a step back. He lifted his cock and showed me the cunt that split beneath it, reached into it with a four-fingered slurp, and came out with a handful of wetness. I swallowed. He reached out to my shoulder, spun me around and shoved me up against the wall, and worked his wet fingers into me. "Convenient, isn't it?" he whispered into my ear. "Hang on, I'll get it all over my cock—" I felt his arm work, then the head bumped against my sphincter.

"Aren't we supposed to negotiate?" I whispered back. "You know, exchanging med records on our chips, that kind of thing?" My cock was hard and I could already feel my asshole wanting it, but I was determined to keep some kind of control of the situation.

He laughed, softly, in my ear. "But that's the point, isn't it? That you don't get a choice? We got you here, to this club, to this situation, to this point in your life. We're even going to explain it to you in a language you can understand, lucky boy."

I tried to swallow again, but my mouth was dry. Must be all that heavy breathing. "Who the fuck are you?" I asked.

He looped a strand of his shirt around me. "I'm the Spinner," he said, and shoved his cock into me. Her cock. Whatever. The world seemed to spin around me, all right, as I got violently fucked up against that smooth industrial tile wall. My hands slipped, but he held me up with a man's strength, cooed in my ear with a woman's timbre in that deep baritone, my ass lubed with his cunt-juice. I remember coming against the cold wall just before he grunted a come into my ass that felt just as cold, like the cold finger that works its way upwards into your gut when you know something's really going to happen.

He pulled out, and my knees buckled. "He's not meant to be with you," the voice said from somewhere above me as I slipped around on the floor, my pants around my knees and my head sliding against my own mess on the wall. "You can't use love as an excuse to avoid your destiny. You know what you have to do."

"I don't want to go back," I grated out, my voice cracking.

"Tomorrow. You know where. We have more to tell you." A light kiss brushed itself onto the top of my balding head, and then there was no one in the hallway at all, just me on my bare and sticky ass in the dark, the silence like a thousand-pound weight pressing in around me.

I didn't want to go back. I had a good, well-paying job out here on this barren corporate island with its artificial parks and stacked apartments. My job paid well enough to rent one of those apartments, and I never went without food. I never ran from the cops. I had a fairly expensive fake identity and even if it couldn't get me a scrutinized security clearance so that I could go with Kevin, it got me a quiet life with a quiet lover, if not Kevin then maybe someone else. I was done being an idealist, a whistle-blower, one of the many tiny scourges of the megacorporate world. They'd swatted me flat with their huge legal flyswatters too many times. I was flattened. I was done. The little guy could go on without me, all right? I'd earned some peace.

I didn't want to go back to that.

I didn't.

Club Fatima was lit with violet lights and had softer music. I looked for the Spinner, but he/she was nowhere to be found. Maybe I could bargain, maybe I could plead, maybe I could get them to see my point. Maybe I could buy my way out. I looked at the middle-aged people dancing awkwardly with each other on the floor, desperate to find someone for the night in the way that the young are never desperate, but no one drew my eye. Then a hand closed on my shoulder, and I turned around to a pair of twinkling eyes.

She was huge, half a head taller than me and enormously fat. Arms jiggled as she raised them over her head, breasts draped over a great belly... or were they man-boobs? At that size, it was hard to tell. She wore a thin fabric tunic that seemed to shimmer with spots of many colors as she moved, over really wide jeans and great stumpy combat boots. Her hair was crew-cut, dyed in several colors like her dress, and multiple earrings decorated her ears. She grinned at me and draped an arm around me. "Don't worry, sweetie," she said. "It'll be okay. It'll all be better than you think." Her voice was a low contralto, womanly but androgynous. Tucking a strand of my thinning hair behind my ear, she went on, "People need you. You know why we can talk to you like this? That's the same why that made you so good at sniffing out the truth. We need people like you in action, honey."

When I'd had messages from the Gods before, they appeared at the edge of my vision and said something that shook me to the core, but that I'm certain I only heard in my own head. They didn't show up in front of me, something I could touch, and fuck me senseless. "Are you the Weaver?" I asked. I had to say something.

She laughed and pulled me to her, ruffling my hair. I could see down her tunic into her significant cleavage. It was covered in hair. She shoved me into it, and I was buried in billowing flesh and furry boobs. "You can't buy your way out of this, honey," she said. "Just relax and take it. That's what you did last night, right? Relax and trust us. Relax, baby. Let Mommy take care of it. Let Daddy take care of it."

I pulled away. "I'm tired," I said. "I don't want to live that life again. I'm older now and I don't have energy. Please. When I was younger, idealistic, I could do it, even face down arrests and jail time." Although it was only a couple of weeks, each time. I knew I couldn't face anything bigger. "I can't now. I just can't. Is there any way..."

She thrust out a double chin. "All right, I'll make you a deal. Get what we're trying to tell you, learn something, and I'll make sure you don't end up in the joint."

"What you're..." I was bewildered. She chuckled again, a rich chuckle that shook all her folds of flesh. "Come on, honey," she said, and backed me up against the wall. *No. I don't want her—too female*—and then she shoved me to my knees, or rather just bore down until I buckled. There were people, but she was so wide that she blocked the whole view. She lifted her great belly with one hand, worked her fly open and pulled out a cock and a pair of balls big enough that only her billowing flesh could have hidden them. "Suck me off, sweetie," she said comfortably, tipping up my chin with one hand and feeding her cock to me with the other.

It was really big, and I choked on it. She made a maternal noise and pulled back, wiped the tears from my eyes, and then shoved it in again, fucking my face. I clutched at her great denim-clad thighs to keep upright. She pulled her cock out and shoved my face below it. "Lick my balls, baby," she said, and her voice was a little deeper, a little rougher. I turned my head sideways and got in there, mouthing each tangerine-sized testicle carefully, then she pulled me back and set me to work on her cock again. "You can take it, honey," she said. "Get that little pud out of your pants and get off. It'll help you suck Daddy's cock. Mommy promises."

I did as I was told, because in spite of everything I was hard. *Again.* I was sure they were doing it to me, but what the hell. This time, the cock in my mouth came before my own, by at least three whole seconds. It tasted like pussy. One ham-fist tucked the equipment back into the baggy jeans, and the other hauled me upright to look up into those twinkling, merry eyes. "Learn anything?"

Yeah. I did. "It's not about women, or men," I said. "It's about me."

A wider grin. "Yeah."

"I don't like being told what to do by *anyone*."

"So choose it yourself," she said, suddenly serious. "Then no one will be telling you what to do." A light touch on my nose. "Tomorrow. One more chance." She—he—turned to go, leaving my mouth dropping open slightly. I wanted to answer—*that's no choice!*—but I couldn't even get it out. As she walked away, I wondered if she was going to vanish like the Spinner, but she just stumped across the room in her combat boots and went out the other door.

Why wasn't the Weaver at the attorney's office, I grumbled to myself all the way over. What the hell? Can't they even get that right... The secretary pointed me to a seat, but I didn't see anyone except ordinary-looking people, easily recognizable as men or women. Or perhaps, now that I had gotten the lesson, they weren't going to appear as androgynes any more.

The door opened and a lean figure came in, a little stooped with age but still tall. I saw long iron-grey hair pulled back in a ponytail, or maybe a braid. Dark eyes glared from underneath shaggy grey brows in a craggy face, lined and seamed to the point where gender was irrelevant. The wide-brimmed leather hat and fringed buckskin jacket, chinos shiny at the knees with wear, they could have been on anyone. One gnarled brown hand, gleaming with blocky turquoise rings, clutched the head of a wooden cane that looked to be carved from a tree root. "Come on." A crook of one gnarled finger. "I'm taking your case. Outside."

We went outside, and I followed this Fate around the corner of the building, to the back. "Don't like being inside." The voice was shrill with age, like a crow's voice. He—she—this time I really couldn't mentally gender them in my head—glared at me and said, "You think it's easy, lining up all those not-coincidences? Getting every little detail right? We did the best we could, you know."

I shrugged. "Don't go to any trouble on my account." *How about forgetting that I exist?*

A snort, then the glare again. "What are you really afraid of, boy?"

No point in beating around the bush. "That it'll kill me. Cutter."

This time, a sly smile. "You're afraid of death, boy? There are a lot worse things than that, you know." One gnarled hand flicked out; there was a gleam of metal in the sun. A knife, one of those cheap fake-turquoise tourist lockblades sold in the desert where I grew up. Just like the one that I used to have when I was a kid.

My eyes followed the glint like it was the head of a striking snake. "Yeah, I know. I haven't even gotten around to those yet. I'm still stuck on death." I sighed. "Look, how can I choose misery and destruction when I don't even know if..."

"You'll ever be loved?" My breath caught, like a punch in the stomach. That wasn't what I was thinking, was it? Yet the words froze me. "I'll make you another deal," the ancient figure said. "Turn away, and someone just might find out about that secret identity of yours. You know that can't last. Satisfy me, and do what you know has to be done. I won't guarantee that you won't die, because any life worth living is a fucking gamble." A pause. "But I'll make sure that you die in love."

The breath hurt in my chest, and I could feel tears blurring my eyes. My lips made several soundless words that never made it out, and then I said, breathless, "Deal." *You know my price, Old One. You know it all too well.*

I dropped to my knees in front of those stained tan work pants and scuffed old boots, but the Cutter poked me with the root-cane and said, "No, lie down. Weeds are soft enough here. I don't like to be inside." I lay down, gingerly, and the cane bounced down next to me. Instead of unzipping a fly, the hand that didn't hold the knife grabbed the tooled belt and shoved the pants down over bony hips, stepped out of them revealing bent, knobby legs. The tails of the wrinkled western-style shirt covered and hid the genitals, whatever they were. The Cutter sat down straddling me with a grunt, and my hard cock—how did it get hard? I didn't even notice this time. Was it when I'd heard that I'd have love?—was enveloped in something, I wasn't sure what except that it was warm and moist and pretty tight. I put my hand up to touch the bony chest under the fabric, and felt a flat, narrow rib cage. Near-fleshless buttocks ground into my hip-bones, but this time instead of being forced I felt like we were partnering, two sides of a dance. We moved together in unison, in harmony. The wrinkled face grunted some more, baring yellowed teeth between narrow lips as I was ridden like a horse. My back was ground into the sand and dirt and concrete tailings, but I kept going doggedly. *You promised me love.*

This time the Fate yelled hoarsely when I was still only three-quarters of the way there, but there was no waiting for me. One hand grabbed the cane and hoisted up off of me, staggering a little, and my cock was left unmoored and still hard. I made a small noise of protest, but the Cutter only cackled at me. "Save the rest for your true love, boy. Now turn your head. Have a little respect for your elders." I closed my eyes, panting, and when I opened them I was alone. I would have masturbated, but I wasn't sure if I should be thinking of a man or a woman. I finally decided that it didn't matter and shoved my softening cock into my pants. It smelled like nothing I'd ever smelled before. *The future.*

In my email the next morning, one of my old friends from before. He's found me. They need me, back home. They'll put me up, send plane fare. It's time.

It's only Fate. I've been screwed by Fate before. And that was just practice, you know. The real thing is so much easier, and so much harder. Bitches come in every gender imaginable.

Lover of the Whore of Babylon

It was my sexual preferences that first attracted His attention; I'm sure of that.

First, I love androgyny in my lovers. I chase transsexuals, male-type or female-type, perfectly willing to say whatever it takes to validate their gender identity so that I can get my hands on their shapeshifted flesh. I will go down on my knees to suck the rubber cock of a stone butch, or the flesh cock of a boy in a dress and satin panties, the skirt lifted delicately to expose the hard-on. I will call it a clit while I'm touching it, like I comment on the nice pecs of the butch whose breast I'm delicately touching. I will shove boy-dykes up against brick walls and lick their freshly shaven heads; I will lick the high heels of drag queens with the same fervor. I don't know what it is, but genderfuck always makes me wet.

But it's more than that. I'm unquestionably a dominant, even when I'm doing things that look vaguely submissive—I'm still running the scene the way I want it, creating my own fantasy and ordering or cajoling the other person to go along with it. I like to be the one in control... but there's a secret part of me that wants to bottom, to submit, to be in the power of someone who could kick my ass, figuratively even more than literally. The problem is that I can't find a human being who inspires that in me. You could be seven feet tall, four hundred pounds of pure muscle, gorgeous beyond belief, the dictator of a small country, with utter self-confidence and a gun pointed at my head, and all I'd be thinking is, "Damn, what an immature fuckhead." On some level, I just can't believe that any human being is worthy to bottom to. I'm sure that drew Him like a fly to rotting meat.

❧

It starts with a visit by my occasional girlfriend. Devi is butch but soft around the edges; she's not stone, and she will let me fuck her until she comes... silently, like a butch. Her athlete's muscles

clench as she rocks with the fucking, my fist cradled inside her.
Her shoulders are broad and boyish; her round ass is feminine. Afterwards, I suggest that I'd like a fucking, and she realizes, to her
horror, that she's forgotten her strap-on.

"That's all right," I soothe her embarrassment, and pull out my
own, along with my box of cocks. I even have an extra harness,
because this isn't the first time I've been in this position. She straps
on the cock that I give her—one of the good things about only
getting fucked by your bottoms is that you can always pick out
the cock—and looks in the full-length mirror on my door, posing
for just a moment, stroking the length of the cock.

Then something happens to her, like a weird flicker running
through her entire body, and she stiffens. "Are you all right,
honey?" I say, laying there on the bed with my legs spread. I'm
hoping that she isn't having some kind of dysphoria problem. It
wouldn't be the first time that I'd held a crying girl-boy or boy-
girl through their pain about not having the right genitalia for
their fantasies.

That doesn't seem to be the problem, however. She turns
around, and the first thing I'm struck with is how damn tall she
seems to be, all of a sudden. The look on her face isn't like her, either. It isn't even Devi-being-someone-else. It is someone else. I
know this, like I know the lines in my own hand. Someone not
human. I swallow, unsure of what to say.

Devi's body walks toward me, with a deliberate stride that
seems wrong, a little awkward but not ungainly. She is walking on
her toes like a ballerina, but her walk seems utterly indelicate. It is
the stalking of a predator, and that's what I see in her eyes. I'm
frozen as her hand reaches out and grips my throat. It's like touching an electric fence, or being hit with a tazer, only there is no
pain. But I can't move, not a muscle. Whatever it is that walks in
her flesh is big, bigger than her, a small crop-haired butch. It seems
to tower over me. He or she? I can't tell. I can only stare, mesmerized, pinned like a butterfly to a paper.

"I'm going to take you now," says the Presence riding Devi's
form. The voice is deep, hollow, caressing in an overly-familiar
way that would make me bridle if it came from a human being.
He—at least I think it may be a He—squats over my face, opens
my mouth with a pinch at the sides of my jaw that makes me

squawk in frightened indignation, and cuts off my squawk with a single thrust of that rubber cock into my mouth.

I'd picked that cock for the size of my cunt; it's too big for my mouth, and I choke over and over as He fucks my face. Tears run down my cheeks, and I feel like I'm going to suffocate before he finally comes, but I still can't move until He finishes with a few thrusts that reach well past my throat muscle. Then Devi's body— His body now, whoever He is—casually climbs off and rolls me over. Out of the spotlight of his gaze, I'm a little more in control, but I still can't bring myself to do more than clutch the pillow and whimper as He shoves lube up my ass. "First the path of Air, then the path of Earth," He says.

There is a moment of quiet, punctuated only with the sound of snaps being undone and done again, and then I am screaming as He shoves the biggest cock that I own up my ass. I've never even had that one in my cunt; it's for my size-queen bottoms. I feel Devi's hand pressing my face into the pillow as He rides my ass, and I sob for each breath, my fingers clawing desperately at the sheets. His cock feels like it is reaching up inside my guts, as if it could grab my careening heart and squeeze it. Devi's thighs slam into my butt with a force she's never used before, and I come hard. I've never come before without my hand on my clit, and it feels as though He is forcing the orgasm into me, up me, out my shrieking mouth and into the air that glitters with his presence.

The cock is pulled from my ass, and Devi's small hands turn me over, surprisingly gently. I stare up into His eyes again, and tremble. *What's happening to me? This isn't me! I'm the sort of cast-iron bitch who doesn't believe in anything, or anyone!*

"One question," he says, as if it is a gift. His smile is evil.

"What are you?" I whisper. As soon as I say it, I know it's a stupid question.

"I am the Lover of the Whore of Babylon," He says. "I am Baptized In Wisdom. I am Rex Mundi. All your darkest places are known to me." While He speaks, His hands dig into my breasts hard enough to bruise. "I am the King of Carrion, the Queen of Clean Bones. I am the Prince of Ashes, the Princess of Graves." He caresses my face, once, and then He is up off me, and Devi is across the room again, looking at her reflection in the mirror.

She turns to me, all shy smiles. "Want to fuck?" she says, as if no time has passed. Then a wrinkle appears between her brows. "Are you all right?" she asks, and I realize that I am laying there with tears streaking my face, my asshole wet and laid wide open, bruised finger-marks on my breasts. I can't explain anything to her without making think that I'm crazy, so I say nothing and just hold out my arms to her.

She fucks me tenderly, sweetly, but I don't come. It's as if all the come in me was used up by His ministrations, and I just end up sending her away.

~

I lie alone for a long time, thinking. Was that real? I could rationalize it, pretend to myself that it was just Devi suffering from delusions or multiple personalities, but I've known Devi for six years and she's as steady and unimaginative as they get, no surprises there. Was it rape? I remember stories of the Greek gods from high school, Zeus raping mortal women. Was it like that for them? Did they just stare into his eyes and go limp, open themselves entirely to him? In all honesty, I cannot deny that on some level, I consented. Some part of me was waiting for this. I nail down that part of my mind, like a worm under a microscope, and stare at it. And hate it. *How could you do this to me?* I snarl inwardly. *You called Him here.*

What if I did? she snarls back. *No mortal man or woman is worthy. Well, He/She is neither mortal nor man nor woman. You know that.*

I know it. I called Him by a male pronoun, but He could be She just as easily. I wrap my arms around myself, shaking like a leaf. *You wanted this. You wanted a top that you couldn't dismiss, couldn't run over, couldn't argue with. Well, you got one. And what will you do now?*

~

I'm dancing in the dark, flickering light of the club. Pretty bodies in black leather and black lace whiz by me, china statues with black lips and tossing hair. I dance slowly, lazily, not really looking for a partner. I'm just here to groove, not to cruise. In fact, I feel a little uncomfortable with the idea of body contact. I think I'd prefer, tonight, to keep my boundaries intact.

My eye passes vaguely over one figure, taller than the rest. She's on six-inch heels, and she looks to be over six feet to begin with. A corset cinches her waist, making an hourglass of her broad shoulders and her perfect, spandexed ass, and she has the long legs that only come on someone who was born a boy. Hormonally modified or just dressing up? I can't tell, don't care; she's eye candy anyway. And then she turns toward me, and her eyes pass over mine.

Just for a moment, I see her soul, human, uncaring, dancing wildly in a club. Then something changes in her eyes, and they lock with mine, and I'm chilled to the bone. It's that presence again, looking out at me. Her expression changes; a cruel and frighteningly familiar smile crawls across her face, and she starts stalking towards me on those high heels. I turn and make for the door, terrified, but then her hand catches my upper arm and presses me up against the wall.

"My little sparrow." A large hand takes me gently by the throat, and I am mesmerized by those eyes like a mouse in the gaze of the snake. "It's so good to see you again," He says, and He bends to kiss me. His tongue invades my mouth, tasting of mouthwash and rot, and one muscular spandexed knee thrusts between my legs and pins me to the wall. I writhe, caught in spite of myself, and when he lets go I feel dizzy and stupid.

He/she lets go of me and turns to walk away. "Follow me," He/she commands, and of course I do. To do otherwise seems unthinkable. Actually, it doesn't even occur to me. He/she takes me out to the back hallway, pins me against the wall again, and one hand rips my skirt up and my underwear down. The other hand holds me by the back of my neck, like a kitten, as He finds my wet cunt—how did it get so wet, all of a sudden! Not fair!—and shoves four fingers up inside me. No foreplay, no warning, just a complete violation. I open my mouth to scream, and He bites down on it, silencing me.

A thumb is added to the fingers thrusting upward, driving me up so hard that I am practically lifted off my feet by the force of the fucking. My cunt stretches painfully—she has such big hands—and I think I feel something tear a little. Sobbing, I climb that tall body with my heels and wrap my legs around her waist, hoping that this will give me some relief, but He just fucks me harder, up the wall until I am hanging by my neck and my cunt, poised and paralyzed. His/her mouth devours me, sucking my tongue out and chewing on it, and the hand becomes a huge fist that punches into me like a piledriver. One part of my brain is still a spectator, marveling at the fact that people seem to be walking past us all unawares, not noticing the mad fucking going on right by the water fountain, and then that thought is lost in the hard come that slams me up and down on that brutal fist by the strength of my own leg muscles.

He lets me down, slowly, until my shaky feet touch the floor; holds me up against the wall by the pressure of His borrowed body until they agree to hold me up. He gently pries my gasping mouth open like one would pry into a pet's mouth to check their teeth, and tucks His wet fingers inside. They taste of cunt and blood. I close my eyes and begin to suck them clean, tears running down my cheeks.

When that large hand is licked clean, fake burgundy nails and all, He removes it and says, "One question." Like before.

You bastard. That's what I want to say, but instead I ask, "Why me?"

He smiles. It could be considered tender, if you could imagine a serial killer trying to be tender. "I like you," He says. "You are drawn to my children. That's a precious thing." Then I am let go, suddenly, and I clutch the wall for support. One hand pushes me down, down to her high-heeled boots, and I kneel there and kiss them. As my lips touch the clunky black vinyl, I have a mental flash of hooves, cloven hooves under my tongue.

Then the boots step away from me, leaving me crouched on the floor in the hallway. Without another word, the tall black figure makes its way back to the dance floor, begins moving to the music. I know that if I tap her on the shoulder, she will not know me, not know that her hand still smells of my cunt and my blood.

I walk into an occult store, not quite knowing what I'm looking for, but it doesn't take me longer than five minutes to find it. In the movies, the old man or woman behind the counter has to pull out a dusty book and look up some exotic bit of lore, but the gum-chewing teenager with the giant pentagram around her neck barely glances at me as I walk in, and doesn't look as if she'd know how to help me if I had demons perched on my shoulders, chewing on my earlobes. It doesn't matter, though, because I see Him—horned, goat-footed, erect cock and open cunt, breasts and hairy pelt. Not the Devil—not part of that world view. Not the Greek Pan, either—too dark, too scary, not male enough. "Who's that?" I ask, pointing to the badly printed picture on the wall.

"That's Baphomet," the chick behind the counter says, cracking her gum, finally looking up at me.

"Is he... like, a god?" I ask, and feel stupid. Of course he is. "I mean, what's he the god *of*?" I try again.

She shrugs. "I dunno. He's not one of the ones that I work with. There's some stuff on him in some of the books... we just keep that picture around for the ceremonial magicians."

I poke at the bookshelves, but an authoritative voice in my head says, *Don't even bother. They don't really know me.* I know that voice, and I stop poking. I buy the picture, take it home, hang it on the wall in a place of honor over my bed. Staring at it, I jerk off. *Are you going to come to me?* I ask. *Or do I have to wait until you feel like it, laying here waiting for your whim? Like any slave laying there, waiting for their master?* The silence is more than an adequate answer. I roll over and weep into the pillow, slamming it repeatedly with my fist. It doesn't help. *Come to me,* I beg, frigging my cunt desperately with my fingers. Nothing. I have no power in this situation, and I hate it. I can't seem to come, either, partly because I'm still too sore from the last time, partly because He hasn't given me permission. When did that happen? I don't remember any such order, but no matter how hard I try, I can't come.

∽

The next night, and the next, the same thing happens. I keep trying, stubbornly; I will not let Him take this away from me, damn it. "What am I doing wrong?" I weep. Finally, on the fourth night, I scream his name in frustration—"*Baphomet!*"—and I am granted an immediate orgasm so strong that I accidentally bang my head against the nightstand.

∽

I have to see Him. I go to a play party, hoping to find a worthy vessel for Him. I dress as submissive as I can, considering that I have a domme's wardrobe. I feel humiliated as I enter—people know me, and they look at me strangely—and I realize that this humiliation is part of what He's doing to me. Straight male tops leer at me and make nasty comments, pleased to see a domina "finally knowing her place," as one says. I ignore them and make a move on a thin, delicate cross-dressed boy with a whip, and then I endure a horribly awkward scene with much enthusiastic and badly-aimed whipping. My god-lover never shows, even when I suck the boy's cock until my eyes water, as if I could suck Him into that piece of flesh through the latex wrapping.

As I lie at home later, nursing my wrap-around welts, the message comes through loud and clear: He will take me at His leisure, when He sees fit and not when I will it. And there is nothing I can do about it. I jerk off four times, picturing Him coming to me in the bodies of beautiful black-haired girl-boys and boy-girls with scarlet lipstick and long nails, their fingers and girl-cocks thrusting into me as I writhe on the floor and lick the rough cleft between the two halves of the hoof planted on my face. In the morning, there is a vaguely heart-shaped bruise across my lips, and I can't remember how it could have happened.

The next day he comes for me, on the train as I go to work. It's early, and there's no one else in the car when a homeless person, wrapped in several filthy coats, comes on. They have stubbly chin hair, but could be either elderly male or female, it's hard to tell. That thought flitters across my mind, and then I feel them sitting down next to me on the bus, the rough coat scratching against my arm. I pull away automatically—don't want to get lice or something—and then the figure clears their throat. The fluttering thought comes to rest in my belly, where it freezes. I look up and see Him looking out of the raddled old man-woman's face.

That face comes close to mine, and I can smell the bad breath. "Did you think that you would be allowed to choose my form?" He hisses at me, and my eyes fill with tears. "All my children are precious," he says. Then he hands me a piece of Saran Wrap and slaps me. "Get down on the floor and worship Me."

And I do, burying my head under three smelly coats and two skirts, pulling down a ratty pair of pantyhose and finding a cunt that reeks so terribly that the tears run down my face as I carefully paste the Saran Wrap over it and lick it out. We stay that way all the way from Alewife to Braintree; I can hear other passengers get on and off, but I trust in His ability to make us invisible, or perhaps I just don't care any more. That grey-haired, crusted cunt convulses about every five minutes, and the wrinkled thighs squeeze my head every time.

Finally He lets me up, wiping off my mouth and kissing me gently on the forehead. "You must not be so taken with appearances," He says to me.

"One question?" I gasp. "Please. Master."

He nods, and I plow on. "Where are you?" I say. "When you're not in a body?"

One hand, in a ratty mitten, strokes my face. "I am always in flesh, somewhere in this world. I am not like the other ones, who live in their own places. This is my world. I live in its time, on its earth. I am never present save in flesh." The dirty wool wipes away my tears. "I am Rex Mundi, King of this World." Then the old body rises, and gets off the bus, and I am left desperately hoping that I can get to a bathroom and get the scent of this encounter off me before I get to my desk at work. My hand goes to my crotch; I'm wet in spite of myself, and I feel like beating the metal wall in frustration.

I am completely undone. I don't try to find Him any more; I just live day to day, hoping that He'll come to me. I wander the streets looking at people, searching faces, asking myself if this one or that one looks androgynous enough to be one of His vessels. Nothing. I go to the bars where the trannies hang out, hoping that I'll get lucky there. Once I swear that he looks across the room at me, through the eyes of one hooker with makeup as thick as house paint, one knowing glance with His familiar evil smile. I immediately rise and hurry to Him, but by the time I get to her, He's gone and she's just a transwoman in a sequined dress looking at me strangely as I drop to my knees. I pretend to have lost a contact lens, to cover my confusion, and I go home crying.

∾

Weeks go by with nothing happening, and I slowly get back to my normal life. One morning I step outside to find the new neighbor, a slight bookish man in his thirties with a receding hairline, struggling with the latch on the laundry room door. I help him out, showing him how to slide it sideways, and we exchange pleasantries. He's shy, blushing and avoiding eye contact, a geeky sort. I deliberately brush against him, flirting, hoping to make him just that much more uncomfortable. I like taunting people. That's why I'm a domme.

It's just one fleeting second, and then He has me pinned up against the wall. I would never have guessed that this nerdy guy might be one of His vessels, and I stutter like a schoolgirl caught cheating. His hand impacts with my face, and he shoves me to my knees. "Crawl, bitch," he says in that smooth voice that seems to ripple through me. So I crawl back to my door, and inside my apartment, and He follows, closing the door.

For the next hour, He beats me until I am begging him to stop, begging him for more. He yanks His trousers down, and shoves my face into a crotch with a wet cunt and a testosterone-enlarged clitoris. I'd forgotten that most transmen pass so well, and it leaves another layer of paranoia and uncertainty on my soul... will I be eyeing every short guy with apprehension now? I suck on His miniature cock for what seems like an hour, His hands anchored in my hair, slamming me against His pubic mound. He calls me His bitch, His whore, His broken angel, His coldhearted cunt that only He could set on fire. "You are on fire, aren't you, little girl?" And I moan that yes, I am on fire for Him and Him alone.

He forces me to fuck myself with things he pulls from my drawers and cupboards—dildoes, food, a rolling pin, a glass tumbler, a shampoo bottle, a pine cone in a plastic bag. I am making incoherent sounds like a beast in rut, repeating "Yes, my Lord!" over and over. I come so many times that it finally becomes painful to come, and he forces me to do it again, on all fours with the leg of a fallen chair rammed up my ass, humping madly while licking his boots. They are ordinary brown leather, but I still feel cloven hooves under my tongue.

At the end of it, I lie in his lap, his hand stroking my hair. "My Lord," I whisper. "Will you ever use me as a vessel?" Somehow I imagine that would be the ultimate intimacy, and the ultimate submission... to give my body over to Him, to use as He would.

"No," he says starkly. "You are only a woman."

I sigh. If that came out of a man's mouth, I'd know that he was saying, *You are only a woman and not a man.* Coming from Him, I know that it means *You have only one gender, one sex; the inside of your head does not resemble Me.* It's the first time that I've ever envied the many genderfuck people I've slept with. As if He hears my thoughts—of course He does!—He says, "You are not one of My children. You are only my lover."

And, I tell myself, it is better than nothing.

I feel the man whose lap I am laying in, naked and bruised, give a start and a gasp, and I know that He is gone. I look up at His former vessel, the poor guy who is probably wondering how the hell he came to be here, and if he's crazy, and if he should flee this place before I press rape charges.

But the look that passes across his face is not one of confusion, just chagrin. "Damn," he says. "He did it to me again."

My jaw drops open. Grabbing his hand, I kiss it; finally someone who I can talk to about this. "Do you believe in miracles?" I ask brokenly.

He gives me a wry smile. "I believe in seven impossible things before breakfast," he says. "And I haven't even had breakfast yet."

I take a deep breath. "I can get you breakfast," I say. "If you'll listen to me." *And, I think, if you'll come by again next week. One never knows when He might want His lover again. Even if I am only one of many, in many places in the world.*

That's the thing about bottoming to an immortal, I suppose. They never run out of shapes. At least, with him, it's not swans and showers of gold. Just my kind of lovers... his Children. His beautiful Children. Be careful when you look them in the eye, when you mock them. Any of them could be Him, staring out at you... and then you'll never be the same again.

Opening

The stone-breaker was just where Rossketil thought it would be, growing out of a crack in what had been a wall in a long-abandoned field. The plague had left many old farms abandoned and unattended, although it had given many riches to the survivors. But instead of buying up and clearing out the old farms, they all rushed to the city to spend their money on frivolities. Rossketil sighed and knelt, feeling the creaking in his bones that not all his herbs could entirely alleviate, and gently extracted the stone-breaker plant. Since the root was needed, he carefully split it lengthwise with his teeth and replanted half of it; in three days he would come back and find out if the half-plant had recovered. If it had, he would leave it for next year; if it was dying, he would take all of it and dry it. One had to think ahead to the next year. Being a *sjaman* meant cropping like a farmer, except that half of one's crops could not be grown in fields and had to be coaxed along in the wild woods on their own merits.

Rossketil hoisted the wicker basket full of herbs onto his shoulder and shook out his skirts—the work skirts, not the ones embroidered with runes and sigils. A *sjaman* of his kind, an *arvegr* one whose nature partook of both male and female in some way, who did not cleave to the opposite sex and produce children, wore skirts to show his nature. No decent man or woman wore skirts; only the *arvegr sjaman*... and the whores. Lift my skirt; I am available to you. It was the whore's message. Only when the *sjaman* wore it, it was not a message to any human being, but to the Spirits. Kicking the mud off of his shoes, he started for home. Perhaps Sibbi would have his lunch ready.

Sibbi was waiting at the garden gate, a worried look on his face. That wasn't unusual; Sibbi was often nervous and anxious. "Spana is here," he said, eyes darting towards the hut. Visitors were kept in the outer room; Rossketil didn't want anyone mucking with his things. It could be dangerous to them, perhaps even fatal.

"What does she want?" Rossketil sighed and handed over his basket. "Get these washed and laid out; I'll deal with them after I've dealt with her."

A shrug. "I don't know, but she's got a woman with her. If she's a whore, she's a new one that I don't know."

"Go on around to the back, Sibbi. You don't have to be around her if you don't want to." Rossketil's voice was gentle and Sibbi's shoulders straightened.

"It's all right; I can be civil to her. I'm past all that. I'm yours now." He flashed a faint smile and made for the back door. Rossketil sighed again and went to the waiting area, where two brightly-colored women were waiting for him.

Spana looked up as he entered and met his eyes with her usual challenging smile. She was dressed in scarlet today, the colors of the lust-goddess Porva Benile; she must have just come from Her rituals. Clouds of sheer scarlet silks embraced but did not conceal her statuesque body; jewels glittered between her cleavage. The *sjaman* kept his eyes away from that cleavage, not for reasons of lust but because he refused to let Spana try to get the better of him. Spana was the priestess of the Nine Love Goddesses, the keeper of the Rose Temple, the mistress of the sacred whores that lived there and exchanged their favors for Temple money. He had a long and ambivalent relationship with her, a decade running now. While the whores were technically sacred beings, the priestesses (and occasional effeminate priest-boy) of the Nine Roses, there was still a good deal of disapproval of them among the more conservative townsfolk, and most doctors refused to treat them when they were ill. Rossketil had no such scruples, and so the Temple was one of his most frequent clients.

However, the first time that Spana had offered him free product as his fee and he had refused, she had been somewhat insulted, and then challenged. She had already noticed that he did not respond to her beauty in any way that a normal man would—Spana might be well past a maiden's age, but she was still stunningly well-preserved—and on his next visit, he was inundated with flirtations from all the whores. He suspected that she was trying to determine his preferences—difficult as he lived alone and had no current lovers, nor past ones in the local town—and was distant and professional with all of them, politely but firmly putting them all off. It wasn't that he found none of them attractive, although he was not fond of any kind of flirtation. It irritated him, and he did not like any assumption that he was a man who could be led around by his balls. But the actual problem was something entirely different.

It made his dealings with Spana into a kind of subtle fencing match, until Sibbi, and then the fat had hit the fire. At any rate, Spana adjusted her veil in a way calculated to show off the attributes that he was coolly not looking at, and said, "Ross, darling! I've brought one of my newest girls to see you. This is Ljufa." She gestured to her companion, a young woman dressed in the rose colors of Nanda, who journeyed to the Underworld. She was pretty enough, not startlingly beautiful as Spana was and could be again sometimes when she wished, but fair in a fragile way with light skin and great clouds of dark hair. She smiled dutifully at the *sjaman*, but her smile quickly faltered. Rossketil had that effect on whores. Spana had still not figured out how, although the answer was clear for the asking if she'd bothered to kneel in front of Qadesh's altar.

He sat down across from them. "What's the problem?"

"For once, not a trouble of the body, dear. She's had some bad times as a child, it gets in the way of her ability to do the work. Leha in town said that you did something for his wife, took away her memory of evil and she could happily share his bed again! Of course, that meant that he stopped coming to the Temple, but I will forgive you for that if you'll help Ljufa here." She stroked the girl's hair affectionately; Ljufa gulped and looked down at her hands, twisting in her lap.

Rossketil looked at her a moment, assessing her and the week's schedule both. "What happened to you?" he asked finally. "Raped by your father?"

The girl bit her lip and shook her head. "My father was a good man," she said. "No, it was my older brother. He ran mad when he was past childhood, and would come into my room and force himself on me. When my father found out, he slew him on the spot, but..."

"The damage was done," Rossketil finished for her, nodding. "Well then. I will need to have you here on the night of the dark moon. Wear no cosmetics, no perfumes, nor clothes that have been drenched in them. Come naked as you were born, only a cloak to wrap you. You may bathe beforehand, but only with plain lye—soap and water. I'll negotiate your fee with Spana later." She nodded, but did not look up; Rossketil feared that he had been too brusque with her. It was often a problem for him; he had no knack with women's feelings. "What we can do, we will do," he said, more gently. Then, wishing that Spana would leave and wanting to get to plant-chopping before the day was past, he rose and bowed briefly.

Spana rose as well. "Come, Ljufa. Let's leave Ross to his work, which is no doubt very important. Oh, and how is that errant servant of yours?" she tossed out just before passing the door.

"My servant is never errant," Rossketil said pleasantly. "He is always entirely reliable. I could never ask for better."

The priestess gave him a look that was only slightly sour and then swept out through the garden. He heard her angry exclamation as her blowing silks caught on the bramblebushes and smiled rather sourly himself. "Dinner," he muttered to himself. "Then I decide what to do with this one."

Sibbi was waiting there, slicing meat and bread, ladling out soup. He had hardly sat down before the dinner was in his hands. Sibbi took his job as servant seriously; his job as assistant even more so. Rossketil studied him over the edge of his cup of soup; his eyes traveled down Sibbi's slender, pretty body, largely hidden as it was by rough work clothes at the moment. A dark fringe of beard showed along his jaw, newly grown in. His hair was long, like Rossketil's own, and so were his delicate, fine-boned hands. They were more calloused now than they had been when he had first come to Rossketil from the brothel; life as a shaman's assistant was rougher than that of a sacred whore. Not that Sibbi ever complained, past that one first time.

He had met Sibbi in passing when he came to doctor the whores at the temple; he was on a first-name basis with all of them. Some could not stop being flirtatious with him, out of habit or wanting to keep some power in the situation, even when he coldly told them to behave themselves. Sibbi never did that. Sibbi was always respectful, even a little in awe of Rossketil, but they exchanged few words. Then, on a grey stormy day that threatened to wash away the north bed of the garden, Sibbi showed up at the gate like a wet, muddy cat with reddened eyes. Rossketil was standing drenched and ankle-deep in mud, trying to dig a trench fast enough to save the peas. *I need to get away for a time, just a few days ... may I stay with you? I'll earn my keep, I promise.* So Rossketil had handed Sibbi the shovel without another word, to see what would happen. The courtesan set to the muddy work with a will, not complaining.

Rossketil had not believed that a whore would ever do such a thing, but Sibbi was a whore like no other, as was haltingly explained that night around the fire.

Sibbi had set out to be useful—filling the woodpile, mending the door, cooking and cleaning. Rossketil had to warn the courtesan what to clean and what to leave alone: *those altars, clean around the things but do not touch them. Those shrines, don't clean. That one, don't even look at; avert your eyes when you go past. The tree with the skulls and the ribbons, don't even go near. These dried plants, crumble them and put them in jars, give them to me for labeling. Those, don't touch. My skirts, my shirts, you can clean; my jacket with the embroidery, leave alone. My belt with the brass circles encrusted with old blood, don't touch. This garden bed is peas; don't pull up anything that looks like this. The herb beds, don't touch.* At night, Sibbi slept on the furs in front of the fire, under an old blanket, a great change from the soft beds at the Temple. A few days turned into a week, and then two; Rossketil did not complain, especially as the house became cleaner and there was more time for him to tend the garden and see clients.

Then Spana came, and demanded to see her runaway. Sibbi hid in the back and begged not to be forced to talk to her. Rossketil was usually impatient with any lack of backbone, but he was moved by Sibbi's tear-filled troubles and sent Spana away: *When he's ready to talk to you, he will. I'll bring him by myself.* She'd screamed at him then: "What a waste! What a fucking waste! If you just wanted to fuck the slut, you could do that at the Temple! I'd give you the pick of the lot for your fees if you weren't too nose-in-the-air to touch one of us save in an examination! And here I thought you were so high and mighty—or maybe that you're fucking impotent, you bastard!—and you steal my bitches away to fuck in squalor, damn you! It's a fucking waste, I say! Curse you and your withered dick, you eunuch!"

Rossketil had summoned his coldest and most deadpan look, waiting in silence until she ran down. There was no point in discussing the reality of the situation, or how wrong she was on any of her points. He simply looked at her as if she was a tantruming child, and eventually she was down to panting and glaring and storming off. Sibbi never asked to visit her and explain, and the sjaman never brought it up again. Instead, he did the magic that Sibbi had finally, haltingly asked him for. The shapeshifting of the whore's body was slow, and required many herbs and much magic, and almost a year. During that time Sibbi fell into being his servant with no complaint. "I'm useful here, at least," he said when

Rossketil mentioned it, after his transformation was as complete as Rossketil's powers could make it.

A bare month after that conversation, one of his Spirits came to him. This was nothing new—the Spirits came frequently and not only when he called them for aid; sometimes they wished something of him. This was a Wind Spirit, one that had been Rossketil's first lover, and he wanted what he always wanted. It was a great and terrible pleasure, as sex with the Spirits always was... but when it was over and the Spirit had taken its leave, Rossketil opened his eyes and saw Sibbi standing in the doorway, eyes and mouth wide.

He knew instantly what had happened. His moans of pleasure had awakened the boy, who had come forth eager to finally, perhaps, offer himself as aid to the *sjaman*'s masturbation. He had offered himself often enough in the months he had been here, but had always been turned down. Rossketil knew what he would have seen—the older man thrashing and moaning in pleasure, the blankets moving in the wind from the open door flap, and the weird glow, the strange feeling of Someone else in the room. The boy would have watched his lips kiss air, then part for an unseen visitor, as would his legs. He had stood there frozen, unable to move, watching, while Rossketil's body bucked and writhed to no visible touch.

"Well," he said finally, as if speaking past a lump in his throat. "I wondered why you always turned me down. I suppose that the Spirits are much better than any mortal. Or was that your wife, and she will not let you stray?"

Rossketil sat up, panting, and patted the furs next to him. Sibbi came over hesitantly and sat down. "No, I am not married to any of them," he said, "although I count a hand's full as my lovers, when they see fit to grace me so. It is..." he shook his head. "Indescribable. But human touch is good as well; the two are simply different."

Sibbi laid his head at Rossketil's feet. "Then let me serve you!" he begged, his voice shaking. "Hnoss at the Temple had a book of stories, of the history of whores, and one of them told of Ysele who was the companion and lover of Kyraakki, the famous *sjaman* woman! I would be Ysele to you, my master. Please, unless you find me... wanting in some way..." He was crying now, and Rossketil put a hand gently on his head.

"You've been reading too many stories," he said. "This is the real world."

"Is there no room for me in your life, in the real world?"

He sighed. "Why? I am not young, or handsome, or—"

"I don't care about that! I'm a whore. Or I was. Now I'm a sja-man's assistant, and I want ... nothing more than to be here. With you. You understand me. No one else does."

Rossketil took his hand away. The boy's hair was very soft. So was his skin. "I had a lover, once. She... could not share me with the spirits. They frightened her. What I must do, to heal people, frightened her." That wasn't the half of it, though. He remembered her face when she had been told what would happen to him, how he would transform, how sex would be from now on with anyone he chose to lie with. "When I was young and the old sjamans trained me—there were two of them—they taught me how the urges of the body could be harnessed to move the spirit, to travel to the Spirits. It does not... look anything like what normal men and women do in their beds. It horrified her, and she left me."

"I would not be horrified," Sibbi said stoutly, laying his head on Rossketil's thigh. The doorflap blew open at that moment, and the wind came in, giving the older man a playful slap. *Don't be a fool.* He smiled, finally, and lay down. "Close that doorflap, would you? We don't need any more visitors. Then come lay down with me."

It was the dark of the moon, and the only light came from the small lantern that Sibbi had brought. Luckily it was warm and windless; the rite of Opening was made much more difficult by cold, and the teasing of the Wind Spirits. One hand clutched a birch twig, a finding-stick. He knelt in the field, knees spread apart, straddling the hole dug between them in the earth. "Hail to Erda," he whispered, "you who take all waste, all that is foul, and redeem it into the green of growing things." Then he turned his thoughts upward, to the stars. Luckily it was a clear night. *Earth to sky. I am a link from earth to sky. Remember that.*

He felt rather than heard Sibbi come forward, standing with the bowl and the bag. Crossing his arms over his chest, he waited, eyes closed.

"Are you ready to be opened?" The ritual question. Sibbi's voice was hesitant.

"I am the horse who will bear the rider. I am open to command." Rossketil's own voice was strong. *It's all right, boy. You know what to do; it's just like every other time.*

"Are you ready to be opened?"

"I am the falcon who will fly and return. I am open to the sky."

"Are you ready to be opened?"

"I am the Door to the Mysteries. I am open to what comes through me." Then he bent forward and laid his face on his crossed arms in the grass. The first time that this rite had been done to him, he had been bound. There was no need for that, now; he was used to the Opening. Sibbi knelt next to him, and he felt those long thin delicate fingers carefully spreading sea-rose-perfumed lard between his buttocks. Slowly, deliberately, they began to work the lubricant into the hole, which yielded to their touch. Sibbi might be awkward around the formal ritual required of him, but he had no hesitation about the technical aspects. The narrow bone tube went in, smooth and polished, and the fragrant, herbed water poured through it, filling him. He panted, the sudden cramps taking him.

"Be thou cleansed," Sibbi said softly, his hand snaking under the *sjaman's* belly to find his genitals. He stroked the older man almost comfortingly, and the pain receded as the arousal grew. Rossketil waited the thirteen breaths and then knelt upright, voiding the herbed water into the hole. "I am cleansed," he gasped, and then lowered his head again. "Formal utterances aside, I think I need another one."

Sibbi made a noise of assent, cleaned him off with a cloth, and repeated the filling and cleansing. Rossketil chanted under his breath, singing the names of the spirits, trying to keep his mind off of the cramps. When he had voided two more bowlfuls and been wiped off again, he crawled forward several feet into cleaner grass. He heard Sibbi with the small shovel, quickly covering the offering of his waste with dirt, filling the hole and returning it to Erda. Then he knelt again by the older man and lubed his asshole yet again, this time more generously. His fingers found their way in deeper, guided by the tensing and releasing of muscles. Rossketil relaxed and let himself moan in pleasure, concentrated on being Open.

As he did, he became immediately aware of the channel that the Spirits had made in him with their brutal lovemaking. It ran up his spine from his ass to the back of his head, and was slowly sphinctering open. If he closed his eyes and turned his vision inward, he could see that astral hole in the back of his head opening, could see the stars through it. In the back of his mind, he could still feel his body rocking, hear his voice moaning. *Sibbi has two fingers in... now three. Now more lard moistened him.*

In bird form, he felt himself rushing through space, through that blackness studded with stars, until the stars ran out and it was just blackness. That was when he could see it in the distance, the huge Tree spinning in space, limned in light, glowing lights hanging in its branches like jewels. He drew closer and alighted in the trees, careful to avoid the glances of the great flying deer that guarded the sacred Tree. Each glowing jewel was a globe of color, like a scene that a skillful craftsman had painted onto the inside of an eggshell, only birds wheeled and branches moved and sunbeams trickled down with swaying motion. *Three fingers stretched his asshole open, and a fourth found its way in. All four were worked in to the second knuckle, gently moving back and forth.*

The topmost one was all blue sky and wheeling birds, calling out in their flights to and forth over shining white towers, their castles just beyond the clouded horizons. *Spirits of Sky, I hail you.* Another one was all glitter and beauty—*Spirits of Light*—and yet another rolled with lush fields, green and golden with ripening wheat. *Spirits of Earth. You are beautiful, but my work here lies lower still.* Past the place of the Spirits of Mountain and Forest, lightning striking over the dark woods filled with strange beasts. Past the Middle Place with the Spirit Serpent, past the realm of the Fire Spirits, all ruby and orange, leaping with flame. Past the realm of the Dark Singers, of the Craft Spirits dwelling in their caves, of the Wind Spirits in their realm of freezing blizzard and great frozen lakes like crystal jewels. Below all of these, at the roots of the great Tree, lay the Land of the Dead. It yawned like a great darkness beneath him, and he left his branch and dived for it. *A thumb now, working its way in next to four fingers. The rhythm was slow—in and stretch the ring of muscle, back out and turn, gently twist back in.*

As he approached the Deathlands, the blackness resolved into twilight, into an autumn glade carpeted with fallen leaves. It was peaceful here, but he had long ago learned better than to allow himself to rest. The eternal peace of the Deathlands could claim you forever if you lay down here. Souls drifted back and forth, ignoring him, the one warm being in this land. He did not see the Lady of the Realm today; the fact that she had not come forth to receive his reverence suggested that She, too, understood the need for haste. He took human form again, as no winged beings were allowed here in this realm. "Find him," he whispered. The birch stick in his hand trembled, and pointed. He shifted into the form of a reindeer, antlers proud in the air, and hurried off across the barrowland. *The stretching had become more intense now, a wave hurtling over him and then receding as Sibbi gently but determinedly worked him Open. His body shook and flushed, pleasure mixed with faint nausea; he groaned particularly loudly as one wave of flushing threatened to bring him entirely back to his body, and Sibbi reached under him and stroked him. The pleasure rose again, and the nausea faded, and the hand in his ass went just a bit further in.*

The birch twig was in his mouth now, both the reindeer's mouth in the Otherworld and his own, lying in the field. It jerked and yanked him, running toward the endless sunset, until he came to one particular barrow that smelled right. Shifting back to human form, he called out, "Open, Dead One! Open, madman! Has death cured you, or are you still mad with a fury of soul, not just brain-fevered!" The earth of the barrow creaked like an old door and gaped a crack. A moan came from it, and it threatened to close again, like a sleeper who has been awakened and desperately pulls the covers back over them. Rossketil struck the barrow with his stick. "Open!" he called out. "Come forth, Dead One! You owe a debt, and I intend to see you pay it!" *Sibbi's hand was in all the way to the knuckles now, his ass stretched to the widest point. His groin throbbed, wanting climax, but he held off. The deed still remained to be done.* "Open!" *his body grunted, as it did so. The hole in the back of his head spiraled wider.*

The ghost came forth. He was not solid like many of the Dead here; his form was tattered and falling apart like mist. That was not a good sign. Some madness was of the body, and it died with the body, leaving a sorrowing spirit who would want to atone for what had been done. Some, though, was madness of the soul, and it traveled from body to body. If left too long without a form, the soul devoured itself. "What do you want with me?" the dead boy hissed.

"You bear something that is not yours," Rossketil said. "You took it from your sister, then you took it to your grave. I want it. Give it to me."

The ghost snorted, and then laughed. "That? That was easy to take, poor weakling. Too easy. Is she still a little fool who could not even fight me?" Rossketil could see him now, an arrogant youth, never grown out of his madness or his adolescence. He had an intuition that this youth had lived other lives, and the madness that dogged him had never allowed him to come to maturity. "No, I will not give it back. It sustains me, here. Why give up so easy a meal?"

Indeed, it might well sustain him, the bit of soul torn from his sister in her extremity. It might well give him a line back to her, to feed off of her fear and pain. *I could force him,* Rossketil thought. *I could attack him and make him give it back. Dead men can be slain; I've done it.* As if he heard the thought, the Dead youth said, "If you try to hurt me, I shall extinguish it. I'll crush it like I crushed her. You'll kill her soul with me, if I go to the Nothing Place." He laughed, his eyes rolling back in his head.

The *sjaman* gritted his teeth. There was only one thing to do, then. "I'll buy it back from you," he said. "I can ask Lady Death to heal your madness. She is the only one who can do it, now."

The Dead youth glared at him. "Why would I want that? Perhaps I like being this way. Anyway, I don't believe that it is possible. I've always been like this..." He laughed, and then just as suddenly threw back his head and howled in sorrow.

"You're in pain," Rossketil said. "Lady Death can take away that pain. I will pay her to do it, if you will give me what I ask. I swear it will be so, on the Nine Deaths and the Nine Roses and the Nine Worlds around the Tree." As he spoke, he glowed with all his Power. *With a final give like a physical sigh, Sibbi's knuckles passed the ring of his ass and the boy's whole hand was buried inside him. His body gabbled nonsense and bucked; the boy's other hand stroked him and brought him inevitably closer to the moment of climax. The ring of stars threatened to engulf the entire back of his head.*

The ghost shied away from him, wavered, howled, finally turned back. "Take it, then!" he cried, and something came flying through the air as if hurled. Rossketil caught it with one hand and placed it in his mouth. It was a stone, smooth and warm, throbbing like a tiny heart. "You promised!" cried the Dead youth, fading back into the barrowmound. "I hold you to it, *sjaman*!" Then Rossketil was sucked back through the blackness, through the Tree, through the emptiness of space, until stars coursed around him. *Sibbi's hand was pumping now, fucking his ass with the rhythm of a horse running, or a reindeer's hooves. Antlered and hooved, he hurtled back through space and into his body just as orgasm crashed over him and he screamed out loud.*

Then it was quiet, except for the faint sobbing that he recognized as his own. The hand withdrew like a snake leaving its hole, and a soft cloth was wrapped between his legs. Sibbi laid a blanket over him and waited, quietly cleaning off his hand. Finally, Rossketil sighed and sat up. A slightly glazed smile spread over his face as he spat a small rock into his hand. "So many stars," he whispered. "Sibbi, get the runes. I will read now, and find out how I must return this to the girl."

∾

The moon was still dark the following night, but it did not matter because this work would be done inside, not in the dark field. Ljufa arrived, nervous and tense in a simple rose-colored cloak. Rossketil sniffed her, pronounced her appropriate, and told her to take off her cloak and lie down. There was a pile of sheepskins in the center of the main room of the hut. No fire; the summer night was warm enough and the hut would likely get warmer still. "Listen to me," he said to her. "If you have us do this, you must swear that you will never tell another living soul what will happen. Swear on the ghost of your Dead brother, and that he might return to haunting you with double the force should you betray us."

Ljufa looked frightened. "I... do not like the idea of such an oath," she said.

He shrugged. "I'll swear first, if you like. That I will do only good for you, that I will not damage you further, that no harm will come to you here. I'll swear on much more dangerous Spirits than a simple ghost, if it matters to you. But if you won't swear, you can go home."

She drew a deep breath, and then let it out. Surprisingly—he did not expect her to trust him without his oath—she said, "I swear, then, by the ghost of my monster brother, that I will keep secret all that is done here—"

"For the rest of your life," he prompted.

"For the rest of my life. And may he come back to haunt me twice over should I betray my oath." She looked stricken as she said it, and her voice trembled, but it was done. He looked at Sibbi, who was waiting with the eagerness of a puppy. "Get ready," he said. "Go ahead." The boy jumped up, tossed away his loincloth, and seized a mass of leather straps which he belted around his hips and between his legs. Donned, they revealed a large leather phallus that jutted out from his pubic bone. He hurriedly anointed it with some of the lard scented with sea-rose, and held out his hands to Ljufa. "Will you allow me to make love to you?" he asked.

Ljufa glanced at Rossketil. "It's all right," he told her. "It's part of the rite. But you are not servicing anyone here today. Just lie back and let him make you happy." Not that she would need that advice, not here, but it had to be said. He watched while Sibbi took her into his arms and kissed her, caressed her, suckled on her nipples until she moaned and swiveled her hips. His lips trailed down her belly and found her cleft, and devoured it hungrily as she cried out, her legs flailing in the air. When she was dripping around his fringe of beard and clutching at his hair, he lay down beside her in the furs and lifted her up, coaxing her onto him. She looked surprised, but straddled him willingly. His deft hands anchored the leather cock in her vulva, now shining-wet and as rose-colored as her dress had been, and she slid down its length with a gasp, her head thrown back and her curly dark hair frothing around her.

The youth seized her round buttocks and moved her up and down on his cock; she was silent, but breathing hard and clearly enjoying it. Rossketil was glad to see her mostly silent; if she had been making artful cries, he would have doubted her sincerity. While Sibbi fucked her, he made sure that he would also have a length of greased hardness for her. Spana did not understand; there was no rule that he could not enjoy sex with others—should they be willing to lie with a sjaman—but it was a tool to work with, not a toy to play with. That was why he swore them all to secrecy, the women—and men, sometimes—who needed a piece of their soul returned. He could feed it to them, but if they were hurt and cold inside, it would not stay. They had to be Open, to be in a mood that would allow the lost bit of soul to slip back in.

Ljufa's breathing grew harder, and her hands went to her pink nipples, which she pinched unmercifully. Sibbi looked over her shoulder to see Rossketil applying grease and stroking a short, thick length between his legs, and the two exchanged glances. The youth tipped the girl forward and spread her buttocks wider, and Rossketil knelt behind her, straddling the boy's darkly furred legs. He ran a hand down her back, so as not to startle her, and his fingers drew a line straight to her pink asshole. She made a noise, then, of surprise, and then a louder one as he began to grease her up.

"It's all right," Sibbi whispered, taking her round breasts in his hands and suckling on the nipples. That loosened her up, and she held still as he opened her with his fingers—as he had been Opened the night before, only not nearly so intensely—and slid into her. Sibbi had stopped thrusting, but as he felt the pressure of cock knocking against cock through the thin tissue of her body, he began again.

They synchronized with each other, Sibbi following him breath on breath just as he'd been taught. Both her holes filled and fucked, the girl began to be much louder. Her gasps became small shrieks, and her eyes closed and did not open. Sibbi, who could see her face and was keeping track of her condition, caught Rossketil's eye and nodded to him. *Close to climax.* He eased their rhythm back down, pushed her forward a little—Sibbi chewed on her nipples to distract her—and pulled out of her ass, just for a moment. In the moment he slipped in the small stone, still warm from his body, and pushed it home by entering her again. It would live inside her Opened body, perhaps for an hour, perhaps for a day, and when she expelled it, it would be merely a stone. The tiny bit of soul inside it would be part of her again.

They speeded up their rhythm again, and soon had her making small crying noises from the double fucking. She climaxed silently, eyes clenched shut, nails digging into Sibbi's stalwart shoulders. Sibbi climaxed as well, a few moments later. He had long ago learned how to climax from the excitement of those he pleasured. Rossketil did not climax. That would happen later, to release the energy. Carefully, he pulled out and let her collapse onto Sibbi. The boy let her lay on him for a moment longer, then gently levered her off to loll on the sheepskins.

She stared up at the *sjaman*, who was squatting back on his heels, wiping his thighs with a cloth. "Something is... different," she said, furrowing her brow. "But I don't know what it is."

"What you lost has been returned," he said. "You brother will no longer thwart you in your bed." Then he looked away from her. It was not good to be too friendly with clients at this moment. They might think that this was more than him simply doing his job. Ljufa turned to Sibbi, who was lying exhausted among the sheepskins. He smiled lazily at her. "Spana told me about you," she said.

"I expect she did," he replied. "I doubt she'll ever forgive me for ruining my market value." He looked at Rossketil and smiled. "Not to mention running off to sort herbs and cook soup and pick reindeer fur out of my underwear."

Her eyes went to the hard leather cock strapped around him. "She told me that you used to be one of the best girls she ever had, but that you... went to the *sjaman* to transform you into a boy." He nodded, not speaking, and she forged ahead. "She also told me that even the best *sjaman* could only make a partial transformation, that you would still be partly a woman."

"Which is why there was no point in me staying on," he said. "The Rose Temple takes few enough boys, and only those with large members. Flesh ones," he said ruefully.

"Why did you do it?" she asked.

"I had to," he said simply, and then shrugged. "That I couldn't choose. This, I could." He gestured around the hut. "It's honorable enough work, given what I am now."

"You know you're bound to silence about all this," Rossketil reminded her. "Don't piss off the Spirits, girl. They'll undo everything we did and make it ten times worse. Unless you want to spend the rest of your life with your brother assaulting you in dreams every night, you'd best keep your word."

Ljufa nodded, eyes wide. "I'll say nothing, I swear!" She watched, blinking, as the *sjaman* unbuckled the straps around his own hips and pulled off the cock strapped to him as well, tossing it at Sibbi's feet. "Go clean these up," he said. "Both of them." Then he grabbed for his skirt and pulled it up over himself. "Sibbi will get you a cloth to clean yourself with," he told the wide-eyed, staring Ljufa. "Then you should be getting yourself back to the Temple." He turned to go.

Her voice stopped him. "Please... master *sjaman*. I must know... Why do you not take what we at the Temple have to give? We would not shrink from you or begrudge you. But Spana says that you never..."

Rossketil sighed. "Do you feel like a whore right now, girl?"

She frowned. "What do you mean?"

"He means the Sacred Veil," Sibbi told her. "The invisible Veil that we put on in order to be sacred whores, that keeps us safe from the clients, that connects us to the Nine Roses, that tells us how to behave, to be alluring..." He trailed off, and corrected himself. "That tells *you* how to behave. I will never return to the Temple."

She nodded. "It is the first thing we are trained in. What of it?" Then it hit her, and she started. "You are right. The Veil is not here for me. In fact, I..." She reached out as if to grasp something, and looked panicked. "I cannot find it at all!"

"You will get it back, as soon as you leave this place," Rossketil assured her. "It is only in my presence that the Veil goes away. One of my Spirits is Mundos, the lover of Qadesh. He did this to me, made it so that in my presence a whore cannot be a whore. That is why I never go to the Temple during business hours, and why I cannot..." He shrugged. "Besides, my sex belongs to the Spirits. Even if I use it with someone else, they might choose to interfere at any moment."

"Which is a true terror, let me tell you," said Sibbi, but he was laughing. At the look on Ljufa's face, he laughed harder, exchanging a glance with Rossketil, who smiled reluctantly in spite of himself. Then the boy jumped up, stripped off his own cock, and beckoned to the girl. "Come! I'll wipe you down, then you can have a hot drink and be on your way." He led her out by the hand. The *sjaman* watched them go, and sighed. *There had better be a hot drink for me, lad, as soon as she's gone. I need it.* The Spirits whispered in his ear; she would be fine now. She would be strong and healthy in whatever she chose. But there was still payment to be made.

~

The next night, the moon was a tiny sliver in the sky, like a curved knife. He leaned against the two poles, bracing himself, naked in the warm night. It was time to pay Lady Death, to buy mercy for the poor mad brother's soul. The first time that this rite had been done to him, he had been bound. There was no need for that, now; he was used to the sacrifice.

Sibbi came up behind him, embraced him. "Are you ready?" he asked softly. The cock strapped onto him was much larger than the one he had used on Ljufa. It poked between the older man's thighs, questing.

"As ready as I'll ever be, lad. Don't choke up on me, now. This has to be done." Sibbi backed away, checked to make sure everything was in order. Rossketil heard the swish of the whip, being tested. He adjusted his stance, set his feet in a more stable position, and waited for the pain.

Gallae

Jadviga was busy heaving rocks when the gods granted his request. Baurux' gang had traveled here from Salona, up the coast and overland to Delmatia, and he had gone with them. Although it was not quite the direction he had wanted to travel in, it was better than taking the Roman roads by yourself, alone and unaccompanied, and not a citizen. That had gotten him enslaved once, and shipped off to the Great City as a slave gladiator.

"Put thirty-one through thirty-eight over there, under the tree," Zagid, the fat owner of this house-turned-rock-pile wheezed. Jadviga sighed and hauled the stones the extra twenty cubits. It was the custom in Delmatia to number every stone in one's house so that when the tax collectors came from Rome, one could take the whole structure apart and then moan forlornly to the tax collectors about how terrible it was here, how everyone lived in grass hovels (hastily erected for the occasion) and how there was no wealth in Delmatia at all. Then, after they were safely down the road, having extracted only a few coppers, one could reassemble one's house as if it was a child's toy, dig up the buried root cellar where all the finery was hidden, and go on with life. Of course, there was a great market for travelers with strong backs to do the actual stone-hauling. Baurux's entire gang had signed up, although Jadviga suspected that it was only a ruse for Baurux's real ambition, which was probably to rob the tax collectors.

He was just taking a break to get a dipperful of water and consider, yet again, if he wanted to have anything to do with attacking a tax man well-guarded by a Roman century when the gods dropped a handful of Fate in his lap. Beyond the crest of the hill a sound began to make itself known; a sound of cymbals and drums and chanting. Zagid perked up noticeably. "They are early this year!" he exclaimed in his gutteral Illyrian accent. "Usually they don't show until after the tax collectors come through and we have rebuilt everything!"

Jadviga had ducked quickly behind a pile of stones. He had learned to do that rather frequently over the past year since his escape. Everywhere he went, he stuck out like a sore thumb— over six feet tall with blond hair and beard, obviously a Teuton barbarian. "Is it the Roman troops again?" he asked from where he crouched.

"Nay, nay, Jadvigus, it is only the procession from Cybele's temple at Mount Ida. You need not hide." The fat man chuckled; he had guessed Jadviga's uncertain status when he had hired him. "They only come to wait for the rebuilding, so that they may bless our new homes and start the sacred hearthfires." He winked at the tall Teuton. "They come every year with their procession, and they never tell the Romans, either."

Something chimed like a bell in the back of Jadviga's mind. "The temple of... Cybele?" he whispered, standing. "The—the gallae?"

"Aye, then you've seen them before? Ah, yes, I forget, you've been to Rome."

Been to Rome indeed, he snarled inwardly. Dragged there in chains and left under a bale of hay in a much-bribed merchant's cart. Rome can be damned as far as I'm concerned. "No," he said slowly, in a accent just as thick in its own way as the Illyrian, "it was before Rome that I saw the gallae. In Cyrene." And I kept the gift I got there ever since, all through the humiliation of my captivity. It kept me from madness. Jadviga's hand went to the small battered leather pouch about his neck on a thong, and remained there as the Cybellines crested the hill.

There were ten of them, ten and a donkey carrying a small golden statue of a goddess in a miniature temple pavilion. Their garments fluttered in the wind; women's chitons and pallae in fine saffron-dyed linen, embroidered flammaem over long, elaborately curled hair dyed with henna or bleached with mares' urine. Jeweled pectoral plates gleamed on their breasts, inlaid with religious scenes and symbols. Their faces were painted with cosmetics; kohl rimmed their eyes and emphasized lashes, and red paint rouged their lips. All ten danced about wildly, flinging their long hair about and chanting in high falsettos at the top of their lungs. A few were pretty enough to be taken for maidens without a second glance; the rest ranged from homely to one in particular who reminded Jadviga of the story of when Thor dressed as a bride in order to infiltrate a giant's stronghold.

Then he saw her, towards the end of the procession. She was trying to dance and shake a sistrum and keep the temple from falling off the donkey with one hand. Something that felt like a great convulsive fist reached up from his belly and grabbed him by the throat. He remembered her from Cyrene. There was no way he could ever forget her.

Her hair had been darker then, not reddened with henna as it was now, and she had been almost painfully thin, without the soft curves that showed under the saffron robes. He had walked into the middle of some celebration that he did not understand, and had been given a quick explanation by a cheering bystander. The gallae had come pouring down through the streets in a frenzy, lashing themselves and each other with braided whips until their blood dripped onto the ground. Townsfolk had knelt in the streets to touch it. Jadviga had stared, openmouthed. "They are seidhr-kraefter!" he had cried out to his native informer, who was busy looking over the shoulders of other bystanders and at any rate would not have understood the barbarian reference. Jadviga knew the godhi seidhr-kraefters, the men who incarnated the corn god and then sacrificed their manhood; if they lived, they were allowed to wear women's clothes and rejoin the tribe as women. But he had had no idea that there was such a custom anywhere else.

The thin boy on the steps of the temple had stood, swaying, hands crossed over his chest. The hair was long as a girl's, hanging forward over the shoulders as he was flogged over and over by two older gallae. The whips were of coarse braided wool with the pastern bones of sheep knotted in, stained pinkish-brown with old blood and new. The boy had been whispering something over and over between moans, but was obviously in that state where pain crosses back and forth over the line to pleasure. The whips fell again and again, leaving welts and cuts across the back, the shoulders, the curved buttocks. A beautiful boy, Jadviga thought, his own manhood growing hard and obtrusive under his tunic. He was not much for great burly men like himself, but boys were just as fine to take pleasure with as women. More, perhaps; they didn't grow big with child and demand you settle down and wed them.

The screaming frenzy of the gallae had reached a peak, as had the screaming of the crowd and the deafening noise of cymbals and drums. The boy was spinning now, frantically, naked under the whips. The other priestesses circled him, chanting. As the chant reached a peak, he was seized and thrown to his knees on the steps. A sharpened pottery shard was thrust into his hand, and his genitals were arranged on the step before him. Jadviga could not look away. The sacrifice of the Ing gods was done privately in a swamp by a priestess of Nerthus, not by one's own hand in front of the entire populace. The boy had raised his arm high, a strange ululating cry issuing from his throat. There was a collective indrawn breath, and then the hand fell with one sweeping motion.

The roar of the crowd was deafening. Oddly enough, the new galla did not scream, but only knelt gasping as if there was no sound left in her slender body. Blood splashed the temple steps, and the gallae fell to touch it and smear it on themselves. The newly emasculated youth tried to rise and failed, and instead held up the severed genitals in one hand and flung them into the crowd. There was an immediate scramble as twenty or thirty people hit the ground looking for the lost piece of flesh. Someone's mule brayed and bumped into Jadviga. He ignored it, watching the new galla's eyes roll up in her head as she fell. A half-dozen priestesses—real women, he noticed—who had been standing unmoved and away from the frenzy descended on her. A quill was inserted into the severed hole and hot, smoking pitch was smeared on the wound to stop the bleeding. She was bandaged with lightning quickness and borne away on a litter, and the last he saw of her was one hand trailing limply from the cloak thrown over her, a hand just a bit too large for a woman's, but much smaller than his own.

He had turned, then, wanting to get away from the riotous scrambling through the gutters near him, and then he noticed something at his feet. It was a tattered, fist-sized piece of flesh. One of the dogs was sniffing it, and growled at him as he bent to retrieve it. He had cuffed the cur, which had slunk off, and hid his new good-luck charm in his cloak as he had stolen out the other way.

Zagid tapped him on the shoulder, bringing him out of his memories with a jolt. His eyes were still fixed on her swaying ass, and his hand still clutched something that had once been a part of her flesh. He turned unseeing eyes to his employer. "Don't gawk, man," the Illyrian was saying, "unless you have gold coin to pay for your gawking. It's only polite to make offerings to the holy ones, and perhaps they'll tell your fortune. Me, I'll wait until the tax collectors have gone by."

The gallae went on down the road through the rubble of the city, and Jadviga tore his eyes from them and went back to heaving rock. His thoughts swirled like fish in a rainbarrel. I am mad, I am doomed, I must have her. I have carried her offering over my heart for nearly four years now. I must have the rest of her as well. But...Baurux wants me to help with the ambush; he's got a backup of Thracian resisters and he needs my help. If I were to take her while the legion was here, the other gallae would make petition and I'd be in trouble. But if the soldiers were occupied by an ambush at the time... Baurux, my friend, you'll have to go on this suicide mission without me.

Grunting, he heaved another stone into place and continued to plan his act of sacrilege.

∽

It was midnight, two nights later, that he crouched at the edge of a small field in the woods. Light from a flickering campfire shone through the open doorway of an abandoned barn. The Cybellines had chosen to sleep there until the houses were rebuilt and a celebration could be declared. The tax collector and his century had come through that morning; the village headman had wrung his hands and whined of how the bandits had taken everything, ruined the whole village, oh, it was terrible, everyone would probably starve this winter and his lordship must come back again next year, if anybody lived. He had handed over a few token coppers and been left untroubled.

Voices filtered through the doorway of the barn, feminine falsetto and masculine giggles. As he crept nearer, he could make out some of their conversation.

"... of course, that donkey's got to be replaced, girls. He's going to fall over any day now! Why, I swear he'll probably choose the middle of the procession to kiss the dust and die."

"And won't that be a poor omen, Glykera! Well, at least we did well enough in Salona that we can get a new one as soon as we find a town where the soldiers haven't bought all the extra mules for their wagons!" "Aye, Delmatia's always fine this time of year. Fulvia! Pass that wine over here, dear. Aach! As bad as the stuff they give the legions, even!" There was a round of giggles and then one robed figure lurched out of the barn. Jadviga shrank back in the bushes. It was the tallest, ugliest one, apparently the leader, with a great mitred yellow cap on her bleached curls. "I must answer nature's call, my dears; wait until I get back before you swill all of that." She made her way, somewhat drunkenly, to the woods at the edge of the clearing.

It gave Jadviga an idea. The gallae were not unarmed; the larger ones had great antique axes and swords that they danced with in procession, but he expected that they knew how to use them. Apparently feminine weakness only went as far as one's safety among these "girls." Even his delicate little galla carried a large cupris knife at her belt. But where there was wine, there would be trips to the tree....

It was over an hour before she came out, a little drunk and a little wobbly, humming to herself. She had left her cupris behind. "Don't get lost, Philomena!" someone called after her, laughing. Jadviga cut around so as to be on her other side, upwind and out of the briers. She was humming to herself, her voice deeper than he expected. She lifted her skirts and squatted over an old tree stump; after her business was done she began to adjust her robes, and Jadviga got her from behind.

She was stronger than he had expected, too, and louder. She got two good squawks out before he managed to stuff enough moss in her mouth to shut her up, get her palla wrapped around to restrain her head and arms, fling her over his shoulder, and go. He had borrowed one of Baurux's two donkeys for the occasion; the bandit leader would not be happy but it couldn't be helped. There were sounds from the barn behind him, questioning calls. Jadviga got himself and his kicking bundle onto the donkey, lashed its tail with a bramble, and sped joltingly off into the night.

∾

Baurux's second cave was deserted, as he had expected. In case of defeat, they had stashed the lion's share of their raided wealth in this secondary stronghold, far from the cave in the crag where the Roman soldiers would pass below. He carried her to the furthest reaches, still struggling—she had scored a painful kick or two to his ribs—and dropped her to light more torches from the one feebly burning in its clay floor sconce. His sword, taken from a bandit he had quarreled with, was on his back; he unsheathed it and tore the palla from her head.

She was ready to jump and strike, but saw the tip of the blade just inches from her face and scrambled backwards instead. "By the Idumaean Mother, you are a cursed fool!" she hissed. "The death of a priestess of Cybele will not go unavenged, by the mortals or the gods!"

"I won't kill you," he said, feeling stupid. It had not occurred to him that she would assume her death. "I didn't bring you here to kill you."

"A barbarian!" She studied him, eyes narrowed. "Obviously you have never seen gallae before, and you mistook us for mere maidens. Let me go now, and I won't have you chopped into pieces."

Jadviga stared at her, letting his eyes linger on the curve of her throat, the feminine curls and the slight lump of her larynx. "I have seen you before," he said. "I know you. I want... to know more of you." The sword tip wavered and lowered.

She stared at him. "You are mad!"

"Ja, I am mad. God-madness, this. Perhaps I have been touched by the pine-cone of the Roman wine-god. He is a galla like you, is he not?" Jadviga grinned at her. The script for this scene had gone entirely by the wayside. He had no idea what to say, or do, to get what he wanted. Nor was he even sure what it was that he wanted, except to hold that slender body close and grunt out his pleasure in it. How do you tell a total stranger that you have been carrying them around in your heart for years, not to mention a mummified piece of their flesh? "What do you want of me?" She was still suspicious, and frightened. He supposed he must seem very large to her.

"Your beauty." He squatted next to her and let the tip of the sword trace its way up her calf. She did not flinch or shrink away, only glared at him. "Your charm. Your grace. If I can have you for an hour, I will have it forever."

She snorted. "You want what all men want."

He laid down the sword—out of her reach—and extended a hand until it almost touched her face. "I am far from my home," he said softly, "and I may never return, and you are the only one in all these misbegotten lands that I have seen and wanted for more than an hour. The only one."

The galla shivered, almost hypnotized. "You... you wanted me, more than a... a woman who can bear children?" Her tone had changed completely, and there was silent pleading in it.

"What use are children to me, far from my home and people? Ja, it's you I want." Just for a second, he saw beyond her brave bluffing to the sheer courage it must have taken to become a creature that, although revered as holy, was not seen as truly a woman or a man. Who did not know what it was to be desired.

Her eyes dropped. "If I give you what you want, will you let me go?" There was almost a faint hope in her voice.

He considered it through the haze of his madness. Much as her wanted to chain her onto the back of that donkey and keep her with him forever, it was not a practical thing to hope for. "I will," he said haltingly.

She smiled. "My name is Philomena, barbarian. And I know what to do for your kind." She rolled over onto her belly and began to hike her skirt.

Jadviga ran a hand up the back of her leg, but she did not respond, being busy with her girdle. "No," he said suddenly. "This is not how I want it." If all I wanted was compliance, I could get it from any whore. He watched her practiced movements as she moistened between her buttocks with spit. You've done this too many times, haven't you, he spoke to her spirit. Spread yourself for an hour with men who did not care that you were wishing it was over, wishing it would never end. "Take off your clothes," he said.

She rolled back over and looked at him. "All of them? But it's cold."

"You'll be warm soon enough," he said thickly. Then he moved to the pile of discarded rubble and dirty dishes in the cave. Next to a brass cauldron still thick with grease from last night's dinner was a length of coarse tow rope. He turned back; her clothes were off, and she sat shivering on the stone floor, legs drawn up to hide herself.

Jadviga took her wrist in his large hand. Philomena resisted a moment when he began to tie the rope around it, but not enough to hurt herself. "I said I would give you what you wanted," she said in an annoyed tone. "Is my word not good enough?"

"Your word is fine," he said, securing both her wrists together and bringing her to her feet. "But your body is not speaking to me. You think I do not know its language, but you are wrong. I know you better than you think." He tied the rope to a tree root hanging down from the ceiling, cut off the rest of it, and secured her feet.

Philomena was turning pale. I have her, Jadviga thought grimly, undoing his broad leather girdle. "What do you think you know about me!" she whispered, never taking her eyes from his belt.

"I've seen enough of gallae to know where they get their real pleasure. And I saw you there, in Cyrene, on the Day of Blood." He lifted his arm in a familiar gesture and whipped the belt cruelly across her rounded buttocks.

She screamed. "You are mad!" she repeated, sobbing. He hit her again, and again. The red welts raised like plow tracks. Then, gently, he touched her between the tiny budded eunuch's breasts. This time her body responded to his hand with fervor, and she drew in her breath. "Please," she whispered. "This ecstasy is for the gods, not for you, barbarian."

Jadviga drew very close to her, stooping until his eyes were level with hers. "Tonight," he said, "I am your god." Then he seized her nipples in his fingers and squeezed them until she cried out, struggling in the bonds. Her body was plumper than it had been, but the waist was still narrow. He ran his hands over it, luxuriating in possessing her, but did not attempt to touch between her thighs.

Philomena was turning her face away from his, hiding in her long reddened hair. "Has no one touched you before?" he asked her in a whisper. "Has no one wanted you?" She did not answer, and in took a moment before he realized that he had spoken in Teutoni. "Let me give you what you save for the gods," he said in Latin, and resumed the beating. She twisted and screamed, louder and louder with each stroke on her back or buttocks, until suddenly she stopped abruptly as if her fear had been choked off. Startled, Jadviga looked at her face. Her eyes were wide open, staring, the pupils great and dark, and looking at nothing.

Then she began to mutter in a language he did not understand. Several languages. Some clear and bubbling, asome rough and guttural. He recognized the iron tongue of the Saxons, High Gaulish and Low, Greek, Phoenician, and others, but could not make out a single word. Awed, he lifted his belt and let it fall, striping her chest in a crisscross pattern. The strange tongues babbled on and on, and she thrust out her thin chest in apparent pleasure. He went back to her buttocks, and she arched her back, body as tense as stone. The sounds trailed off to a low moaning, and then she gave one great shudder and cried out in what seemed to be a climax.

The belt slid out of his hand to the ground and he caught her as she sagged, hanging from the ropes. Jadviga pried at the knots around her wrists with his fingers, but she had pulled them too tight. He let go of her for a moment to pick up his sword and swung it in a clean arc, severing the rope, and then caught her again before she hit the ground. She clung to him, murmuring something in pidgin Latin, and he was suddenly, powerfully aroused.

Laying her gently down, he reached for the cauldron and got a handful of grease. Philomena was still only half in her body and did not resist as he spread her legs and smeared it into the crack of her ass. The flickering light showed the mass of scar tissue between her buttocks and the froth of her dark pubic hair. Jadviga had a queer throbbing sensation in his chest where the leather pouch lay inside his tunic, and he hesitated.

She opened her great dark eyes and looked at him. "Do you still want me?" she whispered.

"Ja," he gasped. "There's nothing I want more." And he found the right place between the cleft of her buttocks and slid into it.

She wrapped her legs and arms around him and held him as he pumped himself deep inside her, burying her face in the blond pelt of his chest.

Afterwards, as she lay curled in his arms, he toyed with her fine silky hair and examined her just slightly overlarge hands in something like wonder. She shifted her position and looked up at him. "You've seen me before," she said. "Where did you say again?"

He stiffened in vague embarrassment. "Cyrene. I was in town on the Day of Blood. I saw you..." He trailed off.

She laughed, a little, and then touched his beard. "So you did. Did it shock you, barbarian, the glory of yielding to Cybele? Of course, I have always had bad luck, and the Day of Blood was no different. The tradition is that a new galla will be sheltered and fed, and given new clothes, by the family whose house her sacrifice is thrown into. But mine somehow disappeared, and I stayed in the temple, and was given the cast-off clothing of a sister that died."

Jadviga was taken aback. "I am sorry; I did not know," he said. He sounded so genuinely sorry that she looked at him from under her veil of hennaed hair.

"It is of no consequence," she said, and then donned a mischievous smile, as if it was a mask. "You make the beast with two backs well, for a barbarian," she said. "What is your name?"

"Jadvigus," he said, giving her the Latinized version. "And are we not beyond such whore's pretensions, you and I?"

She flushed, and sat up. "Since you will be off tomorrow, and I will not see you again, it makes no difference, does it not?"

He studied her, eyes narrowed, as she began to don her clothes. Her gestures were charmingly feminine. "Would you ever consider leaving the service of your goddess?"

"Never." Her tone was impassioned. "It is the only place I belong."

"There is no way I could change your mind, no way I could make you want to be mine?"

Philomena paused in the act of girding her chiton. She was silent and did not look at him, and something sparkled in her eye. "You already have some part of me, barbarian... Jad-vigus. A part no mortal has touched before today."

"That," he said, "is probably true." And he pulled the small pouch from around his neck, undid the knots, and took out the desiccated offering, mummified with salt and Egyptian spices, and held it out to her.

She stared at it a long time, and then looked at him and then at it again, and then she screamed like a cat and launched herself at him. He was taken aback, and overbalanced. She beat on his chest with her not-so-small fists, cursing him, and then stopped, putting her hands on her hips and looking down at her surprised captor. "You," she said, leveling a finger at him, "owe me a new chiton, you bastard!"

"A new chiton," he repeated.

"And a palla. Green. And earrings of amber." At his expression, she burst out laughing.

∽

"And we were so worried, we roused half the men in the nearest house to look for you, and here you were off spreading yourself for this churl!" scolded Glykera. "You are lucky that the soldiers were off fighting bandits, or we would have had to send them to find you, little trollop!" In spite of the words, the tone was affectionate and the huge galla kept hiding a smile. Philomena had her mischievous grin on and would not let go of Jadviga's hand.

"But I have unfortunate news for your friend here," she went on. "This morning, the Romans came back with the heads of the bandit leaders, and they have decreed that all foreigners present themselves and state their reasons for traveling through the area. I do believe they are looking for Thracian spies."

Jadviga groaned. "Odin's wounds! I will have to try for the hills. Perhaps if I can find—"

Philomena laid a hand on his lips to quite him and looked pleadingly at Glykera. "Could we... perhaps... tell the Romans that he is a servant of Cybele, with our temple?"

Jadviga sputtered and pushed away her hand. "I would rather be spitted on a Roman spear than be unmanned!" he protested.

Glykera laughed, dropping out of falsetto into a surprisingly hearty bass. "Foolish man! Not all who serve the temple are gallae. Someone has to take care of the donkeys."

"And this one is so big! Where did you find him, Philomena?" cooed Fulvia, batting her heavily-kohled lashes. "Perhaps if we save him from the Romans, he'll be... properly grateful."

"Come, dear." Philomena tucked her arm into his and drew him inexorably along towards the town. "We'll take care of anything. None of the villagers will gainsay us; after all, we're sacred. And as for the Romans, well, we're the official representatives of one of the official temples of the Palatine hill. After they've gone, and the rebuilding done, we've got a festival to attend to. You wouldn't want to miss that, would you? Especially since there are bound to be peddlars and you still owe me something."

"Odin's wounds and Freya's ass," Jadviga muttered, eyeing the flock of gallae who were clustering around him like oversized fluttering birds, openly flirting. "Ah well, I suppose there's no choice." As he moved off with Philomena, he remembered the advice his father had given him. Be careful what you ask for.

He decided not to finish the sentence in his head.

Historical Notes: In the Roman era, the temple of Cybele was a haven for individuals we would today consider transsexuals. Self-castrated, they lived as women and priestesses, and were one of the more popular faiths of the area. Cybele was originally an Asiatic goddess from what is now modern-day Turkey. Although the common folk greatly respected the gallae, intellectual upper-class Romans were horrified and disgusted by them and passed a law stating that anyone who so mutilated his genitalia could not be a Roman citizen. The word "galla" is the feminized form of the Latin word for rooster, a Roman play on words.

The gallae were fascinated with the use of flagellation and cuttings in order to achieve religious trance. Their festivals always included some form of flagellation—of themselves, of each other, of anyone who offered themselves to the whips. While "on tour", they would flog and cut themselves with knives and swords until they were in altered states and the crowds would shower them with money for their pain.

Many of the trappings of the Cybelline temple were adopted by the Catholic Church. The robe and mitre of bishops and popes is copied directly from the ceremonial costume of archigallae. This story would have taken place at round 160 A.D. in the area we now know as Albania.

Thief of Dreams

It's dusk outside my tiny apartment, and prime time is just beginning in Sexland. I check my listings, download a list into my brain—complete with addresses and personal kinks—and swoop like a bird of prey through the dreams of thousands of people crowded into this huge, stifling city.

Interesting metaphor that, a bird of prey. I didn't actually see one until I was thirteen and rented a nature VR—something fuzzy and static-filled from the local school library about the Southwest—and there he was, a hawk, diving implacably onto the tiny mice of the desert, fate on wings. I think it was then that I decided to become a predator. It seemed the only option that could give me more than a shell of a life.

So my sig is Dreamhawk, and even if the cops knew about me, which they don't, I've left such a twisted trail around the Worldnet that they would never be able to find me. I'm the best there is, better than the Mysters or the Motleys or even Damballah. After all, I have so much more time on my hands.

(You were supposed to hear an ironic twist to those last words, in case your program is cheap and doesn't have those upgrades. After all, I can only assume someone will eventually, at some future date long after my malformed heart has given out, read these diaries and put them into VR format. Pity I can't sell the rights while I'm still alive. People always love a decent villain.)

Number one on tonight's list: Shira MacKenzie, 322 Terrace Road, age 46, who has rented "Torments of the Damned" from Candy's VRama. It's an easy one to step into; I've used it before. Let's see... Miss Mackenzie is a relative newcomer to the city, but she's rented sexvids before, all heterosex, all kinky, all bottom-space. Is she female herself in Sexland, or does she see herself as a boy? Ah, yes, female like her driver's license. Not that I care. Well... I get to play big hulking male Top tonight, it seems. Yummy, yummy.

I slip her code with ease, insert my virus program—invading

her cheap antivirals is like surfing past slow-motion morons—and enter the world of her fantasy. I'm suddenly in a body, tall and muscled, dressed in scanty leather and sporting a huge erection. The scenery around me is an abandoned warehouse. I know the script of this flick well enough to know what I can and can't get away with. "On your knees, slut!" I roar. First things first. Change the hideous dialogue and lukewarm acting.

She cringes. In Sexland she's tiny, with a perfect seventeen-year-old body and fluffy brunette do. In reality she's probably dumpy, middle-aged, and graying, but hell, it doesn't matter here. I grab her by the bouffant and throw her to the floor. Then I twiddle with the program and ropes come snaking out of nowhere, snaking around her. One coils around her breasts in a figure-eight, tightening until they stand out like taut drums. Others knot themselves about her ankles, wrists, and the crease between her dimpled knees and rounded calves. Another spirals around her waist, loop after loop, cinching into a rope corset that brings her body to impossible dimensions. As a final fillip, her wrists are brought up between her shoulder blades and bound to the ropes encircling her rib cage. She gasps and cries out for help, for mercy, writhing in the throes of delicious fear and arousal.

Oh yes, there's one other little thing I forgot about. Her safe word. It would be listed in the VR's entry program, to stop the vid on command. I check it, momentarily; it's "dishwasher." I erase it.

(Oh, please. Did you really think I wouldn't?)

I step forward, looming over her, and grin evilly. "Slut," I say. "Whore. You want this. You want to be beaten and ravished by me. That's why you rented this vid. So get up on those knees and suck me, and it better be good, or else."

She looks taken aback at the mention of renting the VR. This was not what she had in mind, and it puts a notch in her fantasy. I yank her up by the fluffy hair, force her mouth open, and start fucking it. This particular Top character is pretty massively endowed, and the erection seems rather permanent. She chokes and struggles, but I notice that her hips are swiveling. I come in her mouth, shooting out what seems to be a truly unreal amount of spooge down her throat, and then force her to suck my still-erect cock clean.

She's whimpering now, moaning little things like "please, master..." and "... no, master." I let her have her voice for now. There are better things in store, and I want to hear her scream. I hang her from a hook in the ceiling (do real abandoned warehouses actually have all these hard points, I wonder? I've never been in one. Of course, I've never been outside my apartment in eight years) and produce several whips. Not the tacky things provided by the program; I have my own virtual set brought in with the virus. Including one rather terrifying one with six—foot tails interlaced with tiny shuriken.

She sees them and screams. "No! This is just supposed to be a bondage vid... I don't do pain!"

"Then what good are you?" I leer, and select a cat. It lashes across her bound breasts and she screams louder. One, two, one, two, in a neat figure eight. Red welts are coming up beautifully on the artificial skin.

"Dishwasher!" she screams. To her horror, nothing happens except that I change whips and begin to lay into her ass with a different cat, this one braided with small knots. "Dishwasher... oh god, dishwasher," she moans, trailing off into sobs. My erection is still hard and I stroke it, watching her.

I decide to take pity on her. It's not that hard. I invoke my extremely illegal sexual response program and plug it into her set. It keeps her turned on, restimulates the pleasure centers so that a wave of sexual ecstasy accompanies each wave of pain. You could really fuck up somebody's natural responses with this baby. Of course, we'll only use it the one time. I can see in her face that it's working; her moans take on a different quality and she thrusts her ass out for me to work on. Somewhere in the middle of the whipping, she comes—once, then twice.

The ropes on her legs retwine so that her ankles can be spread wide apart. I produce clamps and decorate her with them. Breasts, ass, inner thighs, labia. Then I whip them off, all but the ones on the labia. Those I leave on while I bend her over and fuck her cunt, first with my cock and then with the spiked whip handle. She's coming now, again and again, in a nonstop feedback circuit. Better finish this up now before she gets brain damage. I put her back on her knees and piss in her mouth, a little fillip I add on a whim. "Drink it, slut," I order. "Remember me. You're going to jerk off to me for the rest of your life." And you'll probably never see me again. I have too many other fish to fry.

I create a temporary malfunction in the feeder circuits of her set. She'll find herself, gasping and half-conscious, back in her own living room while I retract my Dreamhawk virus and fly out to catch other prey.

∾

Prey number two: Ms. Jaye Harper. Age 26, 6171 Fleet Avenue number 44, renting "Biker Boys." An all-male video? Yes, and she's costumed for the occasion in the body of a skinny boy-punk. I check her past rentals, looking for the flags I know mean kinky sexvids. (I can get access to the rental lists of every VR store in town in a millisecond.) OK, she's a dyke from the look of it; this must be an experimental foray into the world of boys. No problem.

I'm waiting in the men's room of a leather bar. How cliche. I'm huge and hulking again, with an even more ridiculous cock, almost cartoonish. Boys will be boys. The leathers this time are covering, chaps and jacket and harness and Muir cap, and I smell like I haven't bathed in two days. Handcuffs and a large ring of keys jangle from the left side of my studded belt.

The bathroom door opens and she—no, he—sidles in. Online crossdressing seems to be mostly a matter of men being women (or girls rather; you can imagine the mammoth ex-football players behind the giggly Marilyn Monroe facades). Ms. Jaye is unusual, and I like that. I disable her safeword—Janine, probably a girlfriend's name—and wait, smoking a cigarette.

The boy moves nervously into a stall, unzipping his pants and pissing. The doors on the stalls are of course all broken and don't latch. I move in behind him, hands sliding down over his ass, feeling him flinch with nervousness. Keys hanging on the right, black hanky tucked neatly into right-hand pocket with a leather cock ring snapped around it. Good. This boy's no bondage bottom. "Looking for trade, boy?" I mumble sarcastically into his ear. My hands restrain his from zipping up his jeans.

He draws in his breath. "Only if... only if it's rough trade, sir," he gulps. He presses his ass against the seam of my leather pants. "You think you can take it, you little punk?" I snarl in his ear. He melts against me. I pinion his arms behind him and snap my handcuffs on. He doesn't resist. Then I twist one booted foot around his ankles and jerk, knocking him to his knees. His face almost goes into the toilet, but he rolls aside just in time. I put one foot on the back of his neck and force his face down onto the other boot, leaning against the stall for balance. "Lick 'em good, you little punk. Lick 'em good and maybe I'll beat your little faggot ass." He does as he's told, and enthusiastically, too. I can feel his tongue like a gentle foot massage through the leather.

OK, so maybe he deserves a good beating. Let's see what we

can do with this scene. I yank him up by the back of his T-shirt and hook the cuffs over the coathook in the stall door. Since this is unreality, we don't have to worry about safety issues and nerve damage. His ripped jeans fall down around his ankles and his little punk cock is hard. Wonder if Ms. Jaye likes having an erection. I know I thought it was cool, the day I hacked my first sexvid at fifteen. Didn't get around to trying out cunts for six months, but then I discovered they're just as good.

I go for the switchblade I know is in my pocket and click it open next to his ear. He flinches, but his breathing gets heavier. "Like that, do you?" I mutter, and proceed to shred his T-shirt off him with the blade. He moans when it accidentally touches his nipple and the slightest drop of blood pearls. I'm standing real close to him and I feel his cock rubbing desperately against my leather-covered leg. "Keep that little punk prick to yourself!" I snarl, slapping his face, and turn him around, slamming him up against the open stall door. That's when he notices the other guys in the room—all vidghosts—watching and leering. He hides his face in his arms, but is visibly aroused at having even this unalive audience.

I take off my belt, fold it in two, and snap the leather, making sure he hears it and jumps. Then I proceed to lay into his ass and back with everything I've got. He twists and moans, but stays put, stays the course. Good boy. Good girl. Of course I don't say it, since he didn't come here for niceties, but for brutality. After about a hundred strokes, he's a mass of welts from his shoulders to his knees, with a white handwidth over the kidney area. He's crying now, whimpering. I grab him by the throat and force him to look at me.

"You wanna get fucked, boy?" I hiss. "You want me up your skinny ass?"

His cock, after all of this, is still hard. "Yes, sir," he whispered, his voice cracking.

"Beg for it, punk." My hand grabs his scrotum, hard, and he cries out, but then manages to pull himself together.

"Please, sir, please fuck me," he gasps, and I throw him to his knees over the toilet and unzip my pants. His asshole is warm and tight, and prelubed. I swear, VR is so much nicer than the real world. No wonder I prefer it.

After I've come yet again I haul him out of the stall and toss him over to the other men in the bathroom. They're each equipped to do basic suck-and-fuck, according to the program, and Ms. Jaye deserves a nice gang-bang for her money. I haven't quite got the hang of inhabiting two virtual bodies at once, but I'm working on it, and once I do you can bet all hell is going to break out, honey.

When they're done with her I disappear them and take her by the hair again. I'm going to give her a special treat for taking that beating. I adjust the vid and run my virus through her system, reducing her to her ordinary VR self and me to a slightly feminized version of that big top. My cock vanishes as I bring her head close to it, replaced by labia and clitoris. She gasps, and looks up at me, and before she can wonder too much I tell her to eat me. Which she does, with tears of gratitude in her eyes.

You're wondering how I can change back and forth so easily, without disturbing a central gender identity. Ah well. Gender is all just a game to me, a mysterious set of masks I play with but can never fully understand. Like everything else that has to do with the flesh world.

~

You see, there was once a pretty teenage girl, like the ones I've fucked so many times in Sexland, without ever knowing what kind of flesh faces lived behind them. Only this little girl wasn't smart; no, she played around in the real world, the world of drugs and diseases and pain that can't be banished at the flick of a switch. Did some whoring, got a couple of viruses, got hooked on a few of the new designer head candies. Got pregnant.

You'd think a half-wasted flesh puppet like that would never be able to carry a pregnancy through. You'd think her pimp would have the decency to pay for a frigging twenty-credit shot of Sero-Abortine. But no. Instead she checks into a hospital and squirts out a pathetic lump of plasma. No arms, no legs, no eyes, no ears, nothing in the crotch but a pee hole. And burdened with, of all things, a genius IQ. Of course they didn't find that out until they gave me my first head plug—that's cranial interface to you dweebs—and my life opened up all around me.

Don't get me wrong, now. My life is just fine. I've got full disability pay, nurse machines to take care of that flesh lump while I get on with my life, and best of all, full uninterrupted free access to the Worldnet. Everything you can experience with in the flesh, I can experience here. And ten times more than that. I can be anyone and do anything. If I felt like interfacing with real people I could do that, too. They've offered me a brain transplant to a healthy body twice now, and twice I've turned them down. It's not just that there's a small rate of failure, which would have me dead on the operating table. It's that if I was healthy I'd lose my free access to the only world really worth having. I'd have to get a job and slog through life like all the other assholes. Is the flesh world worth it? I don't think so.

∾

So. Enough ranting. All this has just been killing time until 2 a.m. when Kit plugs himself in. I've been looking forward to his fantasies with bated breath for weeks now, and it's really hard to get me excited about anything. But Kit is such a twisted little fuck that I think I'm beginning to love him. My heart flutters when I think about it.

Kit is a legal contract slave to a very rich corporate executive in Hyde Park. He lives to serve his beloved mistress, and is allowed all sorts of expensive and very fine equipment. He's not allowed to wear normal clothes, use the furniture, or leave the house, but she allows him the use of her first-class VR rig when she's out, in order to keep him occupied. And unbeknownst to her, he imports some fairly illegal sex vids and plays them while she's not looking. If it hadn't been for Kit's expensive tastes, I would never have gone beyond corner-store fantasies.

I surf into Mistress Katherine's system. Her antivirals are excruciating; they took me nearly a month to carve a channel through. I slide in through my special back door, plug into his VR system, and wait with bated breath. As soon as the vid goes into the slot, I'm occupying one of the two main characters. There are never more than two main characters, and Kit gets to insert appearances as he chooses.

I've been this persona before, and I know it well. Tall, dark-haired, stunning, legs that go on forever, and slightly Hispanic facial features. I'm wearing a sleek skinsuit of metallic silver latex. Kit likes latex a lot. Tall, thigh-high latex boots of a matching color, with a knife tucked into them. A whip dangles at the side of the big chunky belt, and on the other side a coil of silky braided copper rope is made into a carefully coiled noose.

I know whose face I wear. It's a slightly idealized version of his owner, Katherine. He's himself, his own sweet kinky self. Every hair on his body is permanently depilated except for the soft cap of black locks, and he's tattooed with floating Oriental drawings, clouds and cranes and blowing butterflies. He did a year of estrogen therapy at her suggestion, just enough to grow pretty little breasts on his slender, boyish frame; they are pierced, like his cock, with gold rings.

He's always himself in these flicks. I guess who he is really is so way out that he doesn't need to be anyone else. These vids, though, aren't really about who he is so much as what he wants. What his darling mistress will never give him.

The secret, you see, is in his fantasy.

∾

Kit is into snuff. He likes to end every one of these nasty little vids dead in the middle of an orgasm. OK, so no one really dies in them; the interface is just cut off automatically, leaving you shaking and panting on the floor. I know, I tried one once. Not my thing, but Kit has an absolute passion for them. He's "died" at my hands a dozen times. His mistress would have a litter of puppies if she knew he was doing this, and with her image as well. Such a secret we have, my darling. I'll keep it well, never fear. I have a vested interest.

(Ah, you say, that's okay, it's only a vid? Nobody really dies? Not bad enough to be illicit? Consider then, for a moment: how do you think they are made, initially? Where do you think the neuroprogramming of death during orgasm came from, hmm?)

I walk toward him, slowly, as if I'm stalking him. He is, as usual, kneeling on the floor, not looking at me. I watch his little tattooed tits heave with anticipation. He wants it bad, this ultimate come.

I stoop and lift his chin with my hand, and he lifts his long-lashed eyes hesitantly. We've dispensed with the roleplaying by this time. I wonder if he has any idea that I exist. "Speak," I say to me. "Tell me what you want."

"Hurt me, Mistress," he says in a whisper. "Hurt me until you can't hurt me any more."

I pull the noose from my belt and loop it around his neck, like a leash. "Come, child," I say, and lead him across the room. We're in Mistress Katherine's dungeon, which is pretty lush as dungeons go. Equipment-heavy. I decide I want to be outside and I run a couple of programs to change the scene. Walls melt like running water and are replaced with bright blue sky, cloudless and intense. Golden sands stretch out around us. Bare trees crown the hill we are standing on. A hawk wheels, cries out, vanishes over the horizons. This is Dreamhawk's secret territory. I wish I could tell him how much of myself I am showing him by bring-ing him here for this communion, how much of a privilege it is.

There are gloves on my hands, metal gauntlets. They are for handling the barbed wire I'm going to tie him to the tallest tree with. He screams, cries out as it bites into his flesh, but does not resist. Thin trickles of blood run down over his beautiful tattoos like a web of red threads. I tie the noose to a limb, taut enough to inhibit breathing, but not enough to suffocate. My special pro-grams are ready, held in my mind like a poker player lovingly arranges his fan of cards. "Do you love me, my beauty, my sweet-ness, my precious treasure?" I croon to him, stroking his face with the gauntlet.

"I love you, Mistress, oh I love you," he gasps. Music to my ears. Until I started coming into Kit's vids, no one ever told me that they loved me. I can mentally edit out the fact that he's saying it to his mistress' face.

I slap him, hard, with the metal glove, rocking him into his barbed bonds, and he screams. "Say it again," I command.

"I love you!" he shrieks, tears running down his face, one side of which is now bruised and purpling. "I love you. You are my goddess. Please, Mistress, please take me home!"

I shuck the gauntlets and remove the knotted latex whip from my belt. It hisses through the air and splats against a tree limb, and he quivers like a harpstring. Then I begin the lashing.

Kit doesn't take a beating quietly or stoically. Not for him the game of clenched teeth and rocklike stance. He abandons himself to it, moaning, screaming, begging me for mercy, begging me never to stop. I whip him until he is a mass of welts, until his tat-toos stand out like repousse work on an ancient stucco wall, painted with the delicate trickles of blood form the barbed wire. The stigmata of sacred perversion, all over.

His cock is hard, thrusting vainly into the air. I stop for a mo-ment and touch it, stroke it, feeling it throb. I want to climb on it, ride him and use it like Kali squatting over Shiva as I have done in the past, but not this time. A selection of small needles appear in my hand, and I thrust one through the tiny fold of loose skin just under the head. He arches back and sobs. Another an inch below it, and another, and another.

Now the finale. The copper rope tautens about his throat, cut-ting his air off, and I bring my arm back, whip at the ready. The strands will tear out the needles, the asphyxia will heighten the sensation, and Kit will come on the pain as he always does, feeling the counterfeit death in the middle of it. He will—SHIT! What the hell—The program flickers and shuts off, sparks explode before my eyes, and the last thing I'm aware of before dark encloses me is the grinding pain than must have been the jack ripped bodily out of my head.....

༄

I'm coming to, now, slowly. It looks a little blurred. The focus must be off. Probably a bad interface. I'm staring up at a ceiling, and my head hurts abominably. White. Acoustically tiled, like a hospital. Did something go wrong with me medically? Did a nurse machine pull my plug? Was that illegal vid wormed with traps? Theories rotate lazily in my mind. Obviously I've been drugged; that fuzzy feeling is reminiscent of anesthesia.

There are two voices conversing next to me, male and female. Female one sounds strangely familiar, but out of the millions of voices I've heard I can't place it. Sounds have an echoing, unclear feel. Will somebody please fix the video and audio on this damn interface? I hate having to make do with lousy equipment. And I'm tired of staring at a vid of some white room.

"All right," comes the man's voice, nearer to me this time. "Let's get him upright." I feel myself assisted to a sitting position by two sets of hands. Are my voluntary motions disconnected? No, I can lift my head, and move my hands, but it's so hard, it takes such an effort. "He's all yours now, Kate," the voice says again. "Let me know if that monitor shows anything unusual. He's had a week to heal, and Sclepivine has speeded the process up nicely."

"Thank you again, John," says the woman's voice, firm and in command. "And I appreciate you helping in a matter of such... discretion."

"Not at all. It's been quite interesting." What the hell are they talking about? The fuzziness is wearing off, but it's still such an effort to speak. "And a way to discharge my debt to you that will be of some good use to society. Good luck, Kate."

Just as my vision is clearing, he leaves the room. The woman though, steps in front of me, and I recognize her with a shock. It's Mistress Katherine. Not her idealized face, but a more careworn version, with a few strands of grey in her hair. She is staring at me coldly, wearing white scrubs, and I can smell her perfume. The room around me is familiar, and yet unfamiliar. It's hung with chains, and eyebolts. The locked door opposite the open one is studded, like a dungeon. Bad set, I think. I could have designed better.

That's when I realize it. The interface isn't bad. It's gone. I'm looking out through real eyes for the first time.

Pure terror and despair rock me. I watch her watching me with grim amusement and realize that I have no idea how not to show everything I feel on my face. I try to speak. Such an effort! "What have you done with me!" I grate out.

"Given you exactly what you deserve, you disgusting little creature," she says in her cool voice. She is beautiful, even now. I can see why Kit worshiped her.

I panic. "Look," I say in desperation, "it was all just fun, breaking into your system. I only did it to play with Kit. I promise I won't ever touch—"

"It's too late for that." She cuts me off. "I have a few questions to ask you, and you will answer. I guarantee that." Her voice is frozen iron. "How long had you been playing snuff games with my Kit?"

I figure I'd better be honest. "About two months. Three or four times a week. Look, it was no big deal—"

Her expression tightens and she slaps me. Hard. I almost fall off the cot I'm propped up on, and only her grip on my hospital gown saves me. She hauls me up and slaps me again. I've never experienced deliberate bodily pain before and I am speechless, gasping. "Speak only when you are spoken to, and then only answer the question," she snarls. "Why did you do it?"

Okay, I'm pissed now. This I'm not going to answer, even if I had one. "Fuck you!" I snarl back.

She does something to me, lower down, and I scream. The pain makes sparks come out in front of my eyes, and there's no way I can stop it, I can't control anything here. Then she lets go, and I fall forward, gasping, wiping tears clumsily out of my eyes. I've never had to deal with tears before.

"Don't—please —" I whisper. "I'm sorry, I won't—Look, just ask Kit. He'll tell you. I never did anything to him that he didn't want—I—just ask him, okay?" I sniffle.

"I wish I could." Her voice is hard. "Kit is dead."

It strikes me beneath the solar plexus like a battering ram. "What?—But the—It was just a vid..."

Katherine's eyes are hard, uncompromising. "He killed himself two weeks ago. Asphyxiation, in his room. There was no vid involved. I was home, and he didn't dare log in." She pauses, and then stabs it in. "I suppose he was trying to recreate your special treatment. Perhaps he'd gotten used to it."

Tears are blinding me now. Oh, Kit, Kit, my precious sweetheart, you little idiot! Why didn't you wait for me? Why didn't you leave this woman for me? But of course, he never knew I existed, never knew how much I loved him. He'd never leave his mistress for a ghost in the machine. Gone. All gone.

Katherine takes a seat, waits until I'm done. I wipe my face on the bedsheet. The helplessness of this body is frustrating. "How did you find me?" is ask softly.

"I ran his programs to find out what he'd been doing, and I found those vids. Then I checked my guards, and discovered I'd been invaded, many times, by a very clever and careful probe. So I used some vids of Kit inserted into the snuff to lure you, make you think he was still there. Then it was just a matter of waiting for you to take the bait, and tracing your probe."

I realized that the last time we'd played, when I'd showed him my secret place, he'd already been dead. And I never knew. Only a bloodless vid with the mind of this cold spider woman behind it, waiting to pounce, hunting the hunter. Kit, my first real love, was dead to me forever.

I blew my nose on the sheet, and that's when I notice my arms. The wrists are tattooed, delicately, with Oriental butterflies. I look at my chest, knowing with terrible clarity what I'll see. Swirls of green and blue float on the small breasts, around the gold rings. "No!" I scream, and launch myself at her.

I'm not used to the clumsiness and effort of a body, and I only succeed in falling off the bed with a thump, tangled in the sheet. "You bitch!" I sob. "You won't get away with this! It's isn't legal! I didn't give consent!"

I hear her voice above me, unmoved. "A surgeon I knew owed me a favor. And you, you're a danger to society. I'm doing them a favor, too, getting you off the Worldnet. Besides, who will know? Kit's still legally my slave. You signed a contract. I can do anything I want with you for another year and a half. Then, well, we'll see. Oh, by the way, I've permanently removed your link."

I put a hand up, feel the shaved head and the healing sutures where Kit's sweet brain came out and my twisted one went in. "But I can't—I'm not—like him, I—" I shut up. I've lost. Will I go mad, I wonder, before she takes her full revenge? My whole world, lost. My power, stolen. I feel her looming over me. Funny how presences have so much more—well, presence—here. I refuse to look up, rocking back and forth on the bed.

"I could have turned you in to the cops," she said. "They'd have taken it out, too, but then you'd have spent your life inside a nursing home with no sensory input, going crazy inside your own head."

She has a point, but I stare stonily ahead.

"Do you want it back?" she asks. "Your link, I mean."

My head jerks up, but I still do not meet her eyes. *Do I? What do you think, you bitch?*

"Depending on your behavior over the next year and a half, I might be convinced to... well, we'll see how much you want it. How much it's worth to you."

I smile ironically and meet her eyes, finally. Does she think I'm going to fall for that? I'm not a submissive. "No," I say. "You'll never do that. I know you too well. Remember," I point out, before she can protest, "I've been you. Frequently."

She glares, and our gazes thrust at each other, like fencing foils. In that moment I swear to myself that she will never break me, never. It would be a betrayal to Kit, who died for me. Then she smiles, a terrible smile, that of the adversary. "I'll leave you for a little while," she says. "You still need to heal up some more before you start your... work here. Oh, and there's a holo box in the corner. In case you want to watch it." I watch as she turns and leaves, locking me in.

I am in mourning, and I wear the skin of my dead lover on my back, like a penance. So she wants revenge, I think. I can beat this. After all, I'm Dreamhawk. Mistress Katherine doesn't know what a dangerous creature she's locked up in here, what cunning and guile live in this twisted brain. She hates me now, but that will change. I know—better than Kit—what makes a sadist love you.

And that's the first thing I'll have to do. To make her love me. And then use her to escape.

I'm Dreamhawk. I'm up to any challenge.

Jack-A-Roe

"What do you think?" Rabinowitz asked her, checking his watch. It was nearly two on a Thursday and he was probably late for his golf game, Rachel thought to herself. "Is it worth taking to an appraiser, or do you care about its value?"

She sniffed and wiped her hand across her nose—damn head cold—and looked at the letter in her hand again. "I wouldn't send for an appraiser if it was valuable, Jonathan. This stuff was sent to me for religious—spiritual—reasons." He lifted an eyebrow and she sighed. "Hell, it's as if your great-grandfather sent you a five-century old shofar from Jerusalem."

The lawyer snorted. "If something like that arrived in the mail, I'd assume it was stolen and return it to Israeli Antiquities before they knocked my door down. But if you don't care, it'll save us all time and money. Four boxes, then. I'll have the other three delivered to your house, and then we'll be free of the business." He hesitated. "I'm sorry, Rachel. I didn't mean to sound like that, not so soon after your great-aunt's death. Were you two close?"

"No... never met her. She wrote the occasional letter from East Germany, but I never talked to her until the Wall came down. Then she got a job with the phone company and started calling all her relatives, all over the world." Rachel grinned at the memory. "Sometimes in the middle of the night. 'Ya, liebchen, talk to Brigitte now,'" she mimicked the accent. She neglected to mention to her pragmatic college friend that Aunt Brigitte managed never to call at two in the morning when she was sleeping, but when she was awake crying over a lost girlfriend or some other disaster, exactly when she needed an objective, sympathetic outsider. It had been on one of those calls that Rachel had impetuously come out to her aunt, and the older woman had unflappably informed her that Aunt Brigitte's mother's sister Lucie had been "one of those, too, so it is only a family tradition, ya?"

She said goodbye to Jonathan, glad that the huge law firm that had handled Aunt Brigitte's American affairs had sent someone she knew. Five boxes, he had said. Full of old things, family heirlooms.

Rachel knew better. Her great-aunt had been a hexe, a witch, one of a coven of several, holding onto the old traditions even in the repression of East Germany. She knew about Rachel's involvement in the women's spirituality movement and had approved, although the political concepts of goddess-worship were rather lost on her. "You make poppets, ya? Nein? I send you letter, show you how, eh? Take the bedsheet from your enemy, cut into a poppet just so high, stuff mit red thread, and vhen dey hurt you, you stick the thorns of hawthorn in—you got hawthorn there in Boston, liebchen?"

No matter how many times Rachel had tried to explain to her about the law of Karma and how spells on others come back to you, it was no use. Aunt Brigitte would just get impatient and fall back into her Prussian German and finally say something like, "You got to protect y'self, after a while you just know vat you can do and cannot, ya?" Oh well. One couldn't expect much from a bunch of old women living in Communist Germany, meeting in old warehouses and repeating a litany they probably didn't even understand, making superstitious spells with poppets to fulfill their repressed and petty fantasies. Still, they were the elders, and deserved respect. That was why Rachel was so pleased that some of the family's ritual implements had been left to her.

Box one contained the letter and list of things—all in German; she'd have to take a dictionary out of the library and translate. It also contained a rather gruesome talisman; a life-size hand sewed out of kid with a small candle stub burnt down on each finger. Sort of a makeshift Hand of Glory, like from the old demonology books. Ick. She stuck it in the closet, on a top shelf. Time enough to figure out what to do with that later.

The phone rang, and it was Johanna, her roommate and younger cousin. "Zack home yet?" she asked.

"No," Rachel chuckled. "Still over at Mark's place. He barely sleeps here one night a week these days."

"Huh." Silence for a minute. Johanna was a dyke too, and an emancipated minor, barely eighteen and in her second year of college. She was brilliant, and argumentative, and adorably boyish, with her close-cropped hair and torn jeans. "Well, leave him a note and tell him I stop feeding his cat for him as of today. I might want to be gone myself occasionally. Met somebody yesterday."

"I'll tell him, and I'll feed Kittyboo myself if he doesn't come home," Rachel promised, and got off the phone. Might as well.

Not like I've had a sex life in almost a year. Seems like everybody in the lesbian community is either taken or celibate. And you never knew if you could trust those bisexuals... Oh well. Such is life. She sighed and went for the cans of cat food.

◦◦◦

Box two through four arrived by UPS the next morning. Uproar of excitement. Shimmer and Dot, her two cats, accompanied by the lethargic Kittyboo, jumped on the boxes sniffing wildly until she shooed them away, opening the first one with a kitchen knife. Box two—the smallest one. Something like a bundle of feathers and nails and twine rolled together. When she lifted it carefully, it unrolled into a long macrame-like thing. The letter said "Eine Hexestrickleiter." Hmmm...some sort of charm, like a Native American medicine thing? The letter continued, saying, "Hängst du ihn in den Schornstein." Huh. Oh well. Next.

Box three—a glass jar with a peeling label marked "Apfelmus" and a rolled, furry bundle. Rachel examined the jar curiously. It looked like brownish Crisco with dark flecks in it. Opened, it smelled like rank vegetation, like green corn or milkweed. "Trinkst du zu fliegen," said the letter. *Better not mess with this until I get that dictionary,* she thought, and put in the fridge.

The bundle was a pair of fur gloves and a small pouch of the same fur. It contained a few wooden disks with strange markings on them. Not even runes or Theban, nothing she could recognize. Rachel sighed. *Here I've been a practicing feminist witch for two years, got half the neo-pagan books in Griffin's Words, and I still don't know what these things are.* Then she recognized something—the fur that the gloves and bag were made of—and shrieked, dropping them.

It was very definitely a gray mackerel tabby pattern.

"Ugh! Oh, Aunt Brigitte, how could you!" The idea of wearing the dead skins of her own cats revolted her. Oh well, she sighed, *what was I expecting? Delicate carved chalices and gleaming jeweled athames? Be realistic.* As she opened the last box—the largest—she studied the letter in hopes of getting a clue on the contents before another nasty surprise greeted her. The only words that she could make out were something about "Die Maske von Tante Lucie." Oh, this had belonged to her lesbian great-great-aunt! Perfect! Talk about herstory. The other women in the coven would die of envy.

The crumpled German newspaper yielded to show a face leering up at her. It was of carved wood, worn and peeling, framed in tails of black horsehair and large curving horns. A fringed goatee of fur scrap adorned its chin and empty eyes stared up at her. She lifted it gently, shaking her head. *Of all things, a Horned God mask that looks like the traditional devil. At least I hope it is Pan or something. Well, I don't think we'll have much use for this in the women's spirituality group. Maybe it'll look interesting on the wall...* There was something else, though, under the newspaper, something furry. *Please, Goddess, no more dead cats. No, this seemed like rabbit fur, soft grey and brown, hanging from a strip of leather with two buckles... must be a belt*, Rachel thought as she shook it out.

It was a loincloth of leather and furs, and mounted on the front was a large phallus, beautifully carved of smooth bone.

Rachel dropped it in disgust. *So that's what Great-Great-Aunt Lucie had for me. A devil mask and a damned strap-on dildo. How patriarchal and tacky. What, did she chase her girlfriends around with it, pretending to be a man? How ridiculous. Just because I'm a lesbian doesn't mean that I use... those. Well, so much for herstory. Damned if I'm going to tell anyone about this.* In a fit of pique, Rachel gathered up the whole thing and tossed it into the closet.

Darkness, close and reeking with fear and sweat and her own wastes. Four walls, rough brick, so close around her that she couldn't lie flat but had to huddle in the narrow space. It's been two days since they bricked me up, and the food is running low. Fear, fear, terror. They hanged them all, Lud said, Mother and Anna and Gerhardt and all of them, and they burnt my mask, oh my beautiful mask carved ten generations ago. Sound of the chickens, clucking in the yard outside, and faint smoke curling from the cracks in the wattle-and-daub chimney. It had been a beautiful autumn day when they had hidden her in here, but now there was rain on the air. Lud and Marta would have to let her out soon; if the pastor and his damned flunkies didn't come by to search the house tomorrow, they probably wouldn't come at all... or would they?

O Queen of Erlfame, O Lady of the Moon, I do not want to die, I am the only of us left! O Horned King, I swear I will make a new mask, a better one, as soon as I am safe, O old gods keep me safe! You are the new Jack-a-roe, Mother said, and when you are old enough you will be the coven Grandmaster, the Man in Black. It is a safety measure. Tongues may be loosened by torture, but never, never have they found the Man in Black, they think he is merely the Devil himself. The Man in Black must never be found, so He is never a man... the Double Mask has a will of its own, my mother said. It finds its own. Oh, Lud, Marta, let me out, I am sick and frightened and I would rather face the pastor than hide any longer...

༄

Rachel bolted upright in her bed, still trembling. Sweat soaked her body and matted her cropped hair. Damn! Some nightmare. Sun was coming through the windows, and the horned mask leered at her from the dresser. The phallus dangled insolently from beneath it. Didn't I throw that awful thing in the closet, she wondered. No wonder I had nightmares, with it staring at me all night. She got dressed quickly, not looking at it, not daring quite to touch it.

As she stumbled out to the kitchen, Zack, her roommate, greeted her with a steaming cup of coffee. "Heard you yelling in there a while ago," he commented. "You OK?"

"Yeah, yeah, I'm all right, just a nightmare," she muttered, sipping at the coffee. "Haven't seen you around in a while. Mark finally kick you out?"

"Nah, just had to feed the cat. So what are you wearing for the party tonight?"

"Party?"

"Remember? Pre-Halloween Gay/Lesbian/Bisexual bash at the Arlington Street Church. Shanna's gig. Costume stuff."

"Oh, yeah." She sighed. "I don't have anything to...No. Wait." She sniffed and wiped a hand across her nose; the head cold was easing up. "You still got that leather gear you bought once when you were dating that dude whatsisface?"

"Rocky? Yeah. Not my thing, I found out. Got the jacket and pants in the closet, only worn twice. Help yourself."

"Thanks. Might as well do something different. I mean, it is a costume party," she rationalized aloud. *That and the silly mask ought to make a pretty good outfit. If I had time I'd go as something more political... like put on a toga and be Sappho, maybe... nah. No time, and besides three people did that last year.* She grabbed some yogurt from the fridge and headed off to her job at the newsstand.

That night, she stripped to her skin and pulled a plain black T-shirt over her head. She was out of clean underwear, so she was reaching for Zack's borrowed leather pants when that carved phallus fell off the dresser with a clunk. She reached out and caught the mask before it could follow, and then retrieved the bone thing from the floor. It felt strangely warm in her hand, not cold as it should have been. Tingles ran up and down her arm. "No," she whispered. "No, I don't want to..." But her hands were moving as if independent of her, buckling the belt around her hips and cinching the middle strap between her legs. The fur was feather-soft against her skin. There was a hard ridge on the back of the area where the phallus was attached; it fitted perfectly between her labia and rubbed up against her clit. She took hold of the cock and slid her hand up and down; it seemed to throb in her grip in spite of its bone-hardness, and she suddenly realized she was wet, very wet. Her clit throbbed with its own beat, and slowly, inevitably, the two synchronized.

She slipped the leather pants on over the soft furs and zipped them up. The jacket shrugged on, and then, tentatively, she picked up the mask. In the semi-dark it seemed to grin knowingly at her. *Step over the threshold*, it said. *Do it. Do it.*

She lifted it to her face and slipped the horsehair—fringe cap over her head. For one moment, her eyes focused at the night sky outside, at the half-moon gleaming through the window, and then the green fire rose from her groin to drown her.

"Hey!" Zack yelled as the leather-clad figure banged out through the door. "Hey, I thought we were going to share a cab! I'm not ready yet—" He lunged for the door, but caught only a silhouette climbing into a taxi under the streetlights.

It has been a long time. I walk the streets, dressed as I once did in the skins of animals. The lights gleam orange and green and the music is pounding as I enter the dance room behind the church, bodies gleaming and glittering and gyrating to the heart-thumping music. Strange, to see a place of my worship on the territory of my enemies, whose ancestors have burnt so many of my priest/esses. Strange, but perfect. The dance is about to begin.

I dance. They dance also, but with wonderment as they gaze upon me. I writhe through the crowd; those I touch become inflamed, ecstatic, filled with the urge to rut, to fall upon each other. The energy builds, and I push it along. Two women squirm together on the food table, between the punch bowl and the potato chips, hands in each other's pants. A young man approaches me, dances around me, offering himself. I accept. At my touch he forgets himself, his surroundings, everything but lust, and goes down on his knees to open the zipper on my leather pants and extract my cock. The crowd around screams in delight and they dance more wildly. I take hold of his head by the curly blond hair as he puts his mouth on my sacredness.

My hips swivel in pleasure. I would like another young man behind me, to press his hardness against my ass and fuck me in mancunt or womancunt while this young one uses his skilled mouth on me. I would like a woman with satiny lips to stand over him and slip her tongue into my mouth while my hands hunt down her breasts, her nipples firm between my fingers. I would like a whole row of witches on all fours, legs spread or asses toward the sky, waiting for my communion as it used to be when I was the bringer of joy. I am the one who crosses all boundaries.

I think about calling to the crowd and getting what I want—I could do it, too—but a man in a uniform approaches, angry. He gestures toward the youth on his knees, whose clever tongue is making me arch my back and growl, and he threatens mayhem if we do not stop. I laugh and make My symbol in his direction. Immediately his member is as hard as mine, harder than flesh is meant to be, and demands excruciating relief. He whirls, stricken, and runs for the bathroom. I laugh again, and come in the pretty boy's mouth, a shower of golden sparks that zap and tingle. He looks up in ecstasy as it runs over his nerve endings like bubbling waterfalls over rounded stones.

A woman approaches me now—sultry, assertive, demanding, dressed in black like a priestess of old. She strokes me, caresses me, and we dance. My hard cock moves between her thighs. She tells me I have incredible balls, to be doing this here. I laugh and tell her I have none at all, which is the truth. She asks if I would like to go to her place before the policeman gets out of the bathroom. I am not worried, since the I know the man is sitting on a toilet seat in tears, beating off again and again into the murky water in a vain attempt to make his erection go away, but I would like to fuck her, so I agree.

In the cab on the way to her place, she asks my name. Jack, I tell her, and find her breasts with my hands. She does not ask any more questions, and soon we are at her house. Upstairs, on the bed, I put my head in her crotch and eat her, licking warm cunt and sucking on her hard clit, and she grabs my head by the horns and bucks her pelvis like a deer caught in a trap. She is fertile; I can smell it. Not in her body, but in her soul. Some part of her waits longingly to be plowed and sown.

So I do it. I bring my knees up and plunge my cock deep into her. She speaks in tongues and claws at my back. It is often this way with mortals. I come again, spraying her deep inside with golden sparks, and in her orgasm she speaks my Name. For that moment, she knows Me.

As I leave to hail a cab, I look up at her window. What child will she bear me, I wonder? As I wait, she sweeps a mess of clutter off the table by the window and plops down a typewriter with a determined air. Rolling in a fresh sheet of paper, she begins.

I smile and return to the dance. The night is young yet.

Morning seeped in through the cracks in the blinds, and Rachel grunted and pulled the covers back over her head. It was too early to get up, and the bed was far too comfortable. As she lay there, she became aware of a vague horniness, of the kind one often got laying lazily in bed in the morning, and she humped the mattress a little, thrusting the cock between her legs into the crack of the blankets. Not quite satisfied, she reached down into the morass of bedding until she felt its throbbing warmth in her hand and began to stroke it gently.

Then, like a bolt out of nowhere, she realized what she was doing and yelped.

"Ohgodohgodohgod," she moaned, scrambling out from under the covers. There was something ironic about that, but her mind had other things to think about. Memories of last night came flooding back. *That man on the dance floor... the one in the bathroom—did I go into the men's room or the women's room or both?—and that woman, the one I went home with, she thought I was... Oh god. She was touching my chest, and never noticed I had breasts. Or did she just not care? What the hell happened?* Her fingers stumbled over the buckles as she undid the belt and tore it off; there was a faint tearing sensation and her clitoral area felt slightly raw. With a muted, wounded noise, she flung the thing into the corner. The phallus was still decorated with a black latex condom, and when it fell it seemed to lie in wait like the head of a coiled black serpent.

The goat-horned mask lay grinning up at her from the night table, a taunting testament to madness.

Rachel rushed, naked and shivering, into the shower and scrubbed herself practically raw with Zack's loofah sponge.

Ohgodohgod what did I do? There was some sort of orgy in the bathroom at the church, and I ohgod I lowered myself onto this guy's dick while he lay on the floor, he was the one who had all the black condoms, and I bent him over the sink and fucked him up the ass, and his friend with the red hair too, and ohgod there was this bald girl who got down on her knees and kissed my ass and ohgod spread my cheeks and licked my asshole and I thought it was worship, was this all a bad drug trip? Did somebody slip me some acid or something? Was it... magic?

Real magic?

She spent the day curled up on the couch in her bathrobe gratefully watching mind-numbing soaps, terrified to go into her room. Her head cold was back, and she was sniffling. At four o'-clock Johanna got home from her class, breezing cheerily through the door. Her eyebrows went up when she saw Rachel. "Shit, honey, you OK?" she asked. "You look bad, like the flu or some-thing."

Rachel sighed. Maybe that was it. The head cold had degener-ated into flu delirium. Still, she wasn't taking chances. "Do me a favor?" she asked.

"Sure, whatever." The brown eyes in Johanna's gamine face were worried.

"In my room... there's some old stuff. It'd be good if you could take it to the trash for me." Now that she had asked, she was a little embarrassed at being caught with anything like that... thing.

"Sure, what is it? I'm just stopping in for a minute though, gotta pack a bag and run, so it can't be a major cleaning job," she cautioned.

"No, no... just something that got left. A mask, on the night table. And a, a belt, I think, made of fur, that she, uh, dropped, in the corner."

"Huh. Not going to return them?"

"No... don't think anybody wants them, not now." Well, that's true enough. She focused in on Wheel of Fortune as Johanna shrugged and went into her room, gym bag casually slung over her shoulder.

❧

Mask. Yeah, there it was. Neat. Old, too. Looked like an antique, Johanna mused. Rachel must be an idiot to throw this away. *Since she doesn't want it, I might just do some research and find out if it has any value.* Making a mental note to check the Harvard library tomorrow, she sauntered over to where the pile of fur and black latex lay and picked it up, drawing her breath in sharply.

So this is what bothered Rachel, she thought sardonically. Someone probably offered to use it on her, and she's such a politically correct prude that she freaked and threw them out. And is probably still processing to Wheel of Fortune. Huh. She peeled the latex off and turned it over and over in her hand, liking the smoothness. *Nice, for a piece of bone, or is it antler? Harder than my four latex ones, but the harness is a lot nicer. Fur is a neat idea. Bet it feels good, too.*

Lifting it to her face, she rubbed her cheek into the softness and inhaled. It smelled of animal, of sex. Johanna's other hand went inadvertently to her guilty secret, the rolled-up sock she compulsively wore stuffed into her underwear. Men's underwear, although nobody knew that except two girls she had fucked in the past year. Who could possibly throw such a lovely thing away? She unzipped her gym bag and tucked both the harness and the mask in, padded them with two T-shirts and her good silk tie.

Rachel kept her eyes fixed on the TV until Johanna reappeared and headed for the door. "All taken care of," the teenager called back to her. "I'll be gone for the night. Get some rest and drink fluids. You'll get over it." There was an amused tone in her voice that Rachel didn't catch, She sighed in relief that it was all over, and she'd never have to deal with it again.

"Thanks," she called after the retreating figure in the bomber jacket and sneakers. "Good luck, Jo."

"I'm always lucky," Johanna called back, shifting the bag from one shoulder to another. It was true. The right stuff always came to her, like a bolt out of nowhere. Almost as if someone was watching, hoping... She shrugged off the feeling and headed toward the bus stop. It was a beautiful autumn day, with just the faintest scent of rain on the air.

One Hundred and Twenty-Two Petals

The ground was rocky and Briony's horse stumbled twice going up the hill. She put out a hand and gentled the gelding, speaking a few quiet words in the tongue that most animals understood. The horse snorted and tossed his mane, but kept moving, being more careful with his footing. *It could be worse, she thought to herself bitterly. I could be on foot. I could be without my armor and weapons. At least he paid for horses.* Of course, these were just regular human-bred mounts, not the faerie horses of the Fey Folk that she was used to. They were slower-witted, and exasperated her, but in the last two days, exasperation had become a state she was getting used to. *Amanita, you bitch, you harpy. I'm hot and tired and in a terrible situation and it's all your doing.*

They hadn't even given her time to pack after her trial, just booted her out the second the penalty geas was set on her. *Then again, full-blooded Fey were notoriously capricious; quick to anger and slow to admitting mistakes. I grew up among them, she reminded herself again. I should know the etiquette. Take nothing they say at face value and watch your back, especially when you're currently a court favorite. Know that there are always those who would set you up and take you down.*

But she had gotten careless; spending the last four years as a soldier in the Fey Legion hired out to fight goblins for the elves, she had lost the instinct for court intrigue. When Amanita's latest captive lover had come to her and begged her to secretly sneak him back to the world of humans—a huge breach of etiquette for Fey, who did not interfere in each other's sordid love lives—she had lost the scent of a trap, and been set up. Bang. Up against the tittering tribunal with their taste for scandal and dirt. Never mind that she had just been made a knight of the Fey. They wanted a punishment that would keep them all giggling for months.

"Since you have such regard for the denizens of Out There," the tribunal head had insinuated snidely, "then you will be enslaved to the first one that looks you in the eye, be he pigherder or undertaker or the village beggar. You must obey their every command until... oh, what say, a year? Three years?"

"Ten years!" "Fifty!" "A hundred!" came the shrieks from the enthusiastic petal-clad courtiers. Briony had stood straight and cold in her black glass armor, disdainfully ignoring them.

"Now, now, let's not be hasty," another put in. "After all, humans don't generally live that long. Rather than a year limit, let's make it until our proud knight has spread her thighs for the lucky sod a certain number of times!" The crowd cheered and shrieked with laughter, shouting random numbers. *Spiteful little bastards,* Briony had thought grimly. *Up until now I'm their precious half-Fey champion, and now I'm to be whored out to humans for their amusement. I knew that the pure-bloods were just the tiniest bit threatened by us, but still!* Defiance turning slowly to leaden despair inside her, she began to mentally cross her only kin and family off the list. *If they think I'm going to come crawling back to them after this is over, they're idiots.*

The tribunal had come to a decision. "As many times as there are petals in a flower!" It was then that Amanita had seized from her hair one of the great white spider chrysanthemums she loved and thrown it at them. No, not a five-petaled wild rose or anything simple like that. By the time the tribunal had elaborately dismembered the blossom and counted out one hundred and twenty-two, Briony knew she was never coming home again so long as these petty Fey ran things in Thialas Ku'hun.

Ahead of her, her employer's horse stumbled and he hauled back on the reins, calling to her and breaking her out of her reverie. "Are you sure this is the best way? If it gets any rockier we'll never make it to Yirrel before nightfall."

The half-faerie pulled her steed up next to his and averted her face while she spoke. It wasn't really necessary, but the habits ingrained in her by the last month of exile were strong. "It'll ease up right over that ridge; I rode through here once with my war company. Of course, we had better horses."

"Yes, I recall you'd told me about your being a mercenary in the Elven Wars," he said. "Perhaps sometime you might like to tell me about it, from your perspective. It's not that I'm nosy, mind; I just need material for new stories every now and then, and war stories are always..." He trailed off, and she could feel him looking at her.

"I will tell you everything I can," she said dully, "whenever you like." Enthusiasm failed to find its way into the statement.

"Ah, well, I suppose it can wait until we have a warm inn roof over our heads tonight." His gaze drifted from her, and he began to hum softly to himself. *Marvelous,* she snarled inwardly. *Now I'll be playing muse to some wandering bard with a pack of ene-*

mies on his tail who was desperate enough to hire one lone Fey in armor to escort him safely from Shaim's Mark to Hassimidik. And I can't even say no.

The bard in question was discreet enough, Briony would give him that. Wrapped head to foot in concealing draperies, a broad-brimmed russet hat on his head to keep the sun off; all that showed was a golden mane of hair to the waist in back and a round, tanned face in front, decorated with a blond goatee and curls of moustache hair at the corners of the mouth. Keen, intelligent green-gray eyes peered from under that large hat, which had been bought in Shaim's Mark and still bore a few bedraggled feathers clinging to the hatband. The eight-stringed kerabaun in its case was slung over his shoulder. Madrigal, as he had called himself—it was the new custom for bards to name themselves after musical terms, he had chuckled self-deprecatingly to her in his high tenor voice—had never taken the instrument off during the ride, nor let go of it during sleep. Briony had watched him curled around it when she had kept watch last night. At least, she thought grudgingly, he hadn't made any moves on her. Of course, that meant that she wasn't any closer to discharging her geas, either. One hundred twenty-two flower petals. Damn that Amanita.

You have to tell him, she said sternly to herself. *You have to tell him before you get to Hassimidik and he pays you your money and tells you to get lost. Thank the gods he hasn't asked you to do anything like rush a pack of bandits, or rob a merchant. You don't know what's behind those green eyes—a murderer, a thief, a leech—those green eyes you inadvertently, stupidly looked into when he roused you from sleep this morning. You've gone and done it now, and after a month of careful avoidance of eye contact with anyone!* Briony studied him guardedly out of the corner of her eye. Not ugly, at least, though utterly without the lean, graceful lines of the Fey. Wide and stocky, from the look of the shape under those draperies, and an inch or two shorter than herself.

Of course, there was also the possibility that, even if she threw herself on his mercy, he would stilll refuse her. And what then? She would have to follow him until he died, enslaved. Her eyes flickered downwards for a moment at the short skirt of glass scales covering her groin. How could she hide it, the evidence of her Fey blood? Humans were notoriously persnickety about such things. Her own father, she'd been told, had been too drunk to notice, but...

"Ehey!" The bard had ridden on ahead of her and paused on the ridge. "I see it! I see the town!" He turned back, adding cour-

teously, "I apologize mightily if I have ever doubted you, milady."
Then he turned his horse and spurred towards Yirrel.

Tonight, she told herself. *Don't put it off. You have no choice. Tonight.*

Fortunately, once they reached the town and found the local inn,
the bard asked her in a polite but nervous voice if she would mind
sleeping in the same room, since the people who were likely to
be looking for him would have no compunctions about sneaking
in windows. "Of course, we could ask for a room without windows," he went on. "But still..."

"Just who are these people, anyway?" she demanded, and then
flushed. It was none of her concern, after all.

He looked secretive and whispered to her that it wasn't to be
discussed in public rooms, so she had followed him upstairs to
the sparsely furnished room—one passable bed, and a wash-
stand—and waited patiently for his reply. He settled himself on
the bed, but removed none of his swathing draperies. "It's a
rather embarrassing story," he began. "The culprit is none other
than my last employer, the Chieftess Jaida of the Hanni tribes.
Are you familiar with their traditions? In particular, how the new
heir is always sired?"

Briony knelt on the floor before him. "I've heard rumors. The
father is ritually killed, isn't he?"

Rolling his eyes skyward, Madrigal nodded. "While the Chieftess is still pregnant, so that the sire's spirit is reborn in the infant.
Except that this time the Chieftess has decided that the sire, whoever he may be, is too valuable to sacrifice, and so she has set up
a simple minstrel and claimed him instead. So now the priests are
after me, drooling to slit my throat."

"Are you sure it isn't yours?"

"Positive. It's impossible, completely impossible. Proving it impossible, however, would probably get me killed anyway, for other
puritanical religious reasons. No, I won't explain that, it's too te-
dious." His green eyes flashed humor at her. "And the worst of it
is, she was interminably boring in bed!"

The fey knight had to laugh in spite of herself. "Well, if we live,
I'm sure it will make a far better story than any of my war tales!"
she chuckled.

The bard's smile softened. "There, that's the first smile I've seen
from you yet. And here I thought the Fey were always full of tricks
and laughter. Shows how much I know."

Her stomach dropped like a stone and her head fell forward, long russet hair hiding her pale, pointed face. The kindness in his tone cut her to the core. "Cruel tricks, and laughter at injustice!" she choked, and then the story came pouring out of her, like rainwater through a parched gully. She did not look up at him until it was done. "So now," she quavered at last, tears streaming down her cheeks, "I must serve you body and soul until the terms are met. I beg you," and she took off her sword and laid it at his booted feet, "treat me with honor and I will do my best for you. I must anyway, but..."

Madrigal had not spoken throughout the entire speech, and as the trailing end of her words were met only with more silence, she looked up in trepidation. The bard wore a bemused expression, and was twisting his hat in his hands. "Er," he began, paused and tried again, "er, well, that does seem like a problem, doesn't it? What a story it will make, though! How many times did you, er, say you had to, ah...."

"One hundred and twenty two," said Briony miserably, wiping her face with the back of her gauntlet-clad hand.

"Oh. Great Kerenyi. And the horrible little spell socked in on me. How simply awful for you."

Surprised out of tears, Briony looked up. "You... you think so?"

He stared at his booted feet, looking embarrassed. "Well, you must find me... er... rather thick and clumsy, compared to your kind." To her continued surprise, she saw that he was blushing. "I mean, I came upon a few naked Fey Folk once, bathing in the woods when I was a child, and I know how lovely you all are. I must disgust you terribly." There was forced humor in his voice.

"Oh, you're not so bad," Briony rushed in. "I've seen lots uglier in humans." She winced as she realized how that must sound. "That is, I... wait! You saw naked Fey! That means you know about..." Her clasped hands went instinctively to her lap.

"That there is no physical difference between male and female Fey," he said nodding. "I did wonder... how you know."

"We just do," she said. "From birth, and we use signals to tell each other. Some change over as they get older, and some never choose at all." Then something occurred to her. "Wait a moment. You can't have sneaked up on Fey. No human is that quiet. They would have—" She broke off. Something odd about him had caught her attention. Two small points of delicate ivory peeked through the blond mane of hair, previously hidden by the wide-brimmed hat.

The bard blinked, stared at the hat in his hand that he had been twisting as if noticing it for the first time, made as if to jam it back on his head, and then tossed it on the floor, sighing. "Oh, well. The damage is done. I should have been more careful. Damn."

"You're a—a—"

"Satyr, yes. Don't look at me like that," he said accusingly. "Our reputation is exaggerated. We're not all rapists and drunkards. Well, since you know, I suppose I can dispense with these." He began to haul off his heavy boots, exposing furred lower legs ending in sharp—looking cloven hooves. "It was killing me, wearing them all the time."

Briony sat back on her heels, her mouth still dangling open. "And here I thought you were human," she began, feeling terribly foolish. "Of course, I've never actually met a satyr before. I've only heard that they've been known to catch Fey and—and force them."

Madrigal started shedding his voluminous wrappings. "I've never had to force anyone," he retorted. The half-Fey knight was so fascinated that she didn't listen to how that was phrased. Under the wraps he was stocky, muscular, broad—shouldered, and very, very hairy. He wore simple leather breeches and a laced leather vest. Golden fur poured over his arms and down his chest between—was it? Briony's eyes widened, not sure if the twin bulges at the top of the laced vest were what they looked like. The bard caught her gaze and gave her a wry smile. "You may as well know it all," Madrigal said. "Yes, I'm female."

The Fey fell off her heels and sat heavily on the floor. "But I thought there were no satyr females! That's the legend!"

The satyr snorted, unlacing her tunic. "That's a human myth. We encourage it, because humans don't treat their women well, and we females pass as men among them. We have two genders; we just aren't built like humans." The vest dropped to the floor and the breeches were attacked next. "Now if I was male, I'd have a fuller beard, no tits, no cunt, great big nuts, and a much bigger shlong." Briony caught a glimpse of pink lips buried in the golden fur and topped with a small dangling pink phallus. "Of course, if Jaida found out, she'd have me strung up."

"How did you... fool her?" Briony could barely speak.

"Kept my clothes and boots on. When people are experiencing incoherent lust, they don't look for details." The bard turned around in a full circle, showing off her body matter-of-factly. "There. That's all of it. You have to take me as I am. Geas or no geas, I'll sleep with no one ever again who will find my true self disgusting. It's not worth it."

The fey knight lifted herself to her feet shakily. She had not expected any of this, especially not the silent pleading for approval in the satyr's green eyes. "You're not disgusting," she said slowly. "Just... different. And difference might be good for me." She began to shed her black glass armor, and the silken padding and body covering beneath it. Naked, she shivered in spite of the heat; the movement made goose bumps appear on her pale, slender thighs and tiny breasts, and the tiny red penis in its fleshy sheath against her belly moved its tip out slightly. The satyr looked at her in undisguised admiration. Briony thought about the sex she had had with other Fey—childlike, quick couplings between friends, almost passionless in their superficiality. "I'm not sure I know what to do," she whispered.

Madrigal flashed her a sudden wide grin. "Leave that," she said, "to me!" The air suddenly filled with a thick, heavy, musk scent. It dizzied her, and also made her terribly aroused. Warm lightning shot through her groin, and she was at once wet and hard, faster and more intense than it had ever happened before. She swayed on her feet, and was caught by the satyr's hairy, muscular arms and lifted to the bed. Why, she's much stronger than I am, she thought vaguely to herself.

It was her last coherent thought. Later, she was never sure exactly how much time had passed in that haze of musk and shameless burning need, but her shyness fell like a cloak. Periodically, she had flashes of self-awareness—the feel of fur against her breasts and belly, the weight of Madrigal's body on her as her thighs were spread and the satyr drove into her hairless opening. She had been worried that a human would be too large and might tear her delicate genitalia, but the small, pointed female phallus was just the right size. Her mouth found a dangling brown nipple on the furred breast above her and tongued it hungrily. At another moment, she found herself with her face buried in thick golden fur with that stiff, slender prong in her mouth, sucking madly, and one hand curled up just under it in wet, musky cunt up to her wrist. Madrigal was moaning and bucking under her hand and mouth, her large strong hands holding Briony's russet head firmly in place.

At still another moment, she found herself on hands and knees with her buttocks in the air, panting and growling for all the world like a Fey hound in heat as the satyr smeared thick, wet drippings from her own furred cunt into the crack of the Fey knight's taut ass. Then, as if it was the most natural thing in the world, the bard gently spread her ass and slid into her smaller opening. Briony was

so relaxed that there was no pain, only excruciating sensation—
or perhaps she was incapable of feeling pain in this dreamlike state.
She felt large hands calloused from the kerabaun slide under her
belly, one seeking her small breast and hard nipple, the other gently stroking her thin, hard penis. She had long since lost count of
orgasms; the tiny dribble of liquid that spewed from it as she con-
vulsed once more in climax seemed to be the last of her will,
milked from her until she was a heap of compliant, used flesh.

Later, though, after it was over and they lay together in the bed,
breathing softly into each other's shoulders, she realized that her
will was back with her. Testing the fresh memories of sensation as
one tests a sore tooth with her tongue, she wondered exactly how
she felt about it. Used? Fulfilled? What exactly had happened there,
anyway?

The green eyes met hers as she turned her head. "It's the
pheromones," the bard said softly. "We give them off when we
get turned on. They have that effect on humans, Fey, elves, trolls—
not so much on each other, though. It's... sort of a natural weapon,
like skunk scent, but with a different effect." She looked away, her
voice light and false. "I suppose now you'll feel raped, and blame
me. It wouldn't be unexpected."

She made as if to move out of Briony's arms, but the Fey held
onto her. "Don't, please don't!" she cried. "You made it good for
me, very good. I might have been all awkward and shy and ruined
it for both of us otherwise. It was different, but..." She looked
down at their bodies entwined, so opposite, slender pearly hairless
flesh against tanned, golden-furred muscles damp with stickiness,
large hairy breasts against small smooth ones. The movement of
the now-soft phallus against her sheathed rod. Some things, perhaps were not so different. "One hundred twenty-one is not so
much, maybe." Her hand ran over Madrigal's shoulder. "You have
such strength. Why haven't you ever learned the sword?"

"You really think I'm strong?" She looked pleased. "I never
thought about being a warrior; always afraid that my hands would
be damaged. Musicians, you know...."

"I can teach you," Briony mumbled, rolling over on the bed.
"Tomorrow..." Her voice trailed off and she fell asleep.

When her breathing had become smooth and even, the bard
sat up and took her kerabaun out of its case, tuned a stray string,
and strummed a few searching chords. There was the geas, wound
around the little Fey like an invisible thread. The key of B made it
vibrate, C more so, D—ah, there! Madrigal was not a bard for

nothing. The spell twanged like a taut string, resonated to her chords. Briony moaned and twisted in her sleep. Up an octave to high D, up another octave, hold it, again, again—and there was a small snapping sound, a whine, and Madrigal felt a hot lash-like sensation across the back of her hand.

She put her kerabaum aside and shook the Fey knight gently by the shoulder. "Briony, my dear, would you please go jump out the window?"

"No," mumbled the half-asleep Fey. "That's silly."

"Very good, dear," said the bard, patting her shoulder. Just then there was a shriek and a crash from outside, and Briony came fully awake in moments.

Something hard slammed into the door. Naked, she grabbed her sword and advanced. Madrigal scrambled to her hooves on the bed, back pressed against the wall. Another slam, and the door broke open; two armored warriors in tribal tassels and turbans burst through. Behind them, the innkeeper was shrieking, "Not in my place! Not in my place!"

One of them rushed her with a shortsword; she had the longer reach and slashed his arm. Whirling, her sword cut through his hamstrings and then took him down. Speed, not strength, was the Fey attack form. The second took a cut in the leg, stumbled, swung, and narrowly missed her head. He was fast, and skilled, and she was naked. Damn.

Behind her on the bed, the satyr aimed a high kick with her hoof at the back of his head. The thin metal helm caved in, as did the back of his skull. He looked surprised, and fell over. No sooner had he hit the ground than the innkeeper ran in with the lantern, shouting, "Brigands! Help! Brigands!" The light of the lantern fell on the satyr, who stood hopping on one hoof and cursing on the bed in all her hairy naked glory, and the innkeeper's cry turned to "Demons! All the gods help us, demons!" and fled.

Briony lowered her sword and wiped a hand across her brow, whistling her relief. Madrigal grabbed for her clothing and boots, dressing fast. "That did it," she said. "I'll have to leave now. When they start yelling about demons it usually means I'm in trouble. Some trick one of my ancestors played, I'm sure."

"Fine. We'll travel slower now anyway, now that those idiots have been taken care of." Briony reached for her clothing and armor. The half-dressed satyr put out a hand and stopped her.

"You don't have to go," she said quietly. "I broke the geas. It was sloppily done, anyway. Learned how in bardic university last semester. I'm on summer vacation. Now that I'm not being chased—and I doubt they'll keep it up after this—you owe me nothing. Go free and in peace."

"Free and in peace," the Fey knight breathed, struck into still-ness by the realization that it was all over. The bard donned her hat, boots and voluminous wrap. She turned at the doorway, paus-ing as if unsure what else to say.

And where would I go, Briony thought to herself. Not home, certainly. I don't have any friends, not there. "Wait," she said around the lump in her throat. "You—you might still need pro-tection. After all, who knows what might happen?" Catching her breath, she rushed on. "And anyway, I think we could maybe have... fun together. For a while, at least," she added. "Assuming you didn't wear me out so badly I couldn't even lift a sword."

The bard's face split into a grin of—was it relief? "Thank Kerenyi! I was worried I was going to have to sniffle all the way back to Has-simidik by myself! Come here and kiss me, you silly faery."

Blushing, Briony let herself be embraced. Madrigal's moustache tickled her lips and chin, and she felt those calloused hands reach back to grab her ass and squeeze it teasingly. The musk scent rose again, just a little, and the Fey felt slightly dizzied again, but Madrigal stepped away and the feeling ebbed. "I don't have time to ravish you again, but as soon as we find some nice soft bushes far away from here—"

"But—but—we just—" Briony began, but her new friend chuckled and cut off her surprise with one last caress.

"I am a satyr, after all," she said with a wink. "Now get dressed and we'll get out of here before they come back with the priests and I have to rape the exorcist to get us some privacy!"

Bridge Over Shifter's Chasm

One a.m. in the library, and my stomach grumbled. I dug around to look for a snack, and found that I'd eaten them all, so I went down to the cafeteria. Well, actually, it's just the second-floor kitchen; there's nothing cafeteria-like about it and I don't know why Zephyrus bothers to call it that. Maybe because it makes this place sound more like a compound, like a bunker or something. Instead of a badly converted office building with blasted empty lots all around it. But there was a fridge, and a pint of Ben & Jerry's that only had a few bites out of it, and that was good enough to fortify me for another few hours of research.

The place was dead empty. Oh, Zephyrus was up in his cocoon, in some kind of telepathic trance, communing with his dead boyfriend. He wouldn't be up for hours. I briefly fantasized him getting it on with his invisible dead-boy, his body twitching in its shiny white metal tube. Did he ejaculate? Did the dead ex solidify in the tube with him, or was he only present in Zephyrus's mind? Probably the latter, since our esteemed Boss never invited him to dinner with us or anything. We wouldn't have minded, and maybe Manifesto could have seen him. But no, the Boss just moped around dramatically, gluing his hand to his forehead and continually mourning his lost love.

Still, he owned the place, and he fed, clothed, and allowanced the whole team, from the active members to the staff mutants like myself. He was the Boss, and if it weren't for him we'd be having to find real jobs, something which the more mutated of us weren't likely to be able to pull off. He paid for our medical care (which meant quivery-voiced old Dr. Meegran with his opaque glasses, in hiding for some medical-experiment war crime decades ago that we all knew better than to ask about), our uniforms (for the active members, anyway), and our vices, if they were cheap ones. Mine were cheap. I wasn't stupid. A few plants in my tiny former-storage-closet bedroom in the basement, and lots of books, most of which I could justify for the library.

Not that I was a real member. No, that was for the folks with the really great talents... or at least the ones that were better than

mine; our house Team wasn't exactly world-class. I found some
chips and a can of ginger ale left over from the team Christmas
party and smiled. Jackpot. As I stuffed my face, I remembered the
first time I came here. There had been an ad about superhero au-
ditions—OK, Zephyrus wasn't so tacky as to say it in those words,
but it was close—and I wandered over, more out of curiosity than
any certainty I could get in.

There were lines of people in costumes—shiny and skintight,
clunky and metal, swirling and iridescent—and while there were
a lot of tacky half-assed kids with one stupid little talent, and a few
sagging oldsters still trying to look fierce, I could see a decent number of real toughs. Steel-eyed, hard-bodied, looking like they could
rip your head off and shit down your throat, maybe not even using
their hands. No way was I going up against that. I picked up some
literature laying on the table, badly formatted stuff about Zephyrus
and his ideal future team, and thumbed through it. I noted the
grammatical errors and the complete lack of ability to make a
blockquote, not to mention the way they'd spelled "caliber" with
two A's. On impulse, I pulled a red pen out of my pocket and
proofed half a dozen different trifolds, making notes about how
they could look so much more professional, if only... Across the top
I wrote, "Hire me and I'll make these look good." Then I walked
past the long line of toughs waiting in front of the receptionist,
and handed them to her. "Show this to your boss," I said.

Ten minutes later I was in Zephyrus's office, and twenty minutes later I was hired, while the line of superheros outside hadn't
moved an inch. Yup, that's me, the Big Z's mutant copyeditor,
churning out literature and articles and websites and all sorts of
propaganda to spread across the Interwebs. The research I'd been
doing in the library wasn't for some big scientific project. It was
for the company newsletter, which I had to put out every month
and it had better be interesting and amusing. I was catching up on
my work while everyone else was home with their families over
the holidays. Well, the ones who had families, anyway. Manifesto
was off on a jaunt to some mysterious third world country to do
research of the type I *wasn't* doing. Lupita was running somewhere
in some wild place where she didn't have to take human form for
days, and would probably come back with hair like a rat's nest and
the worst breath in the world. Lupita wasn't too bright; she was
just muscle. Zephyrus kept nagging her to change her name. "But
it means wolf," she'd say, staring at him blankly.

"It sounds like somebody's green-card cleaning lady!" he'd say, exasperated. Zephyrus wasn't the most politically sensitive of people, having unfortunately grown up entirely too rich.

Her expression wouldn't change. "But it means wolf," she'd repeat. I bit my tongue and didn't point out that Lupita's mother *was* probably somebody's green-card cleaning lady. Anyway, she was off, and so was Geist. Geist was enormous and humorless and could probably strangle a rhinoceros; he had no friends, communicated in grunts, and was usually parked in his room in front of the satellite TV when off duty. But occasionally he went off to enjoy a bender and probably trash a bar, so I was alone in the place, except for the semi-comatose Boss upstairs. That's why it was half a miracle that I saw the shadowed figure darting through the hall.

I froze as soon as I saw it, ducking back around the corner and holding my breath. The only Team member here who moved like that was Stiletto, and she was only about five feet tall. And she wouldn't be skulking around the hallways. I braced myself and took a quick glance around the corner again, and there I saw her. Tall and lean, with what I refer to as Female Superhero Body Type Three—small-breasted and athletic, just muscled enough that you couldn't call them delicate. The fluorescent light from down the hall reflected off of her orangey-gold skin, patterned like tie-dye. She wore no clothes, not even boots; she didn't need to. Her legs ended in shiny bootlike feet; I expect that she'd hardened the skin for protection. She had no body hair, either, and the hair on her head looked like it was made of fringed skin. It probably was.

I knew who she was, of course. We'd all been briefed on the various members of enemy Teams and Houses; there were files on all of them upstairs in the library. I'd had to write articles on them, fergodssake. Her name was Chimera, and she was a shapeshifter. She could look like anyone she wanted; could pass right down to the voice and skin details, although mannerisms were somewhat harder. There were a dozen or so shapeshifter-mutants of various kinds; she wasn't the most dangerous of the lot, being only a minor member of a major Team, but she was nothing to sneeze at. Frankly, she could probably kill me on sight. The fact that she'd gotten past all the nothing-to-sneeze-at perimeter guardian machines meant that she was that good. The best thing I could do in this situation was to run, sound the alarm, and try my best to wake up Zephyrus. Maybe I could call into town and see if Geist wasn't too drunk yet. This one was so far out of my league that I would be a fool even to let her see me.

I wasn't tall, or muscled, or even fit. I was short and paunchy and very, very hairy, especially on the lower half. Actually, I was entirely furred from the solar plexus down, right down to the hooves. Yep, hooves. Cloven, too. And horns, about eight inches long. Did I wear clothes? Damn straight I did, and a hat too when I went out. Which clothes I wore depended on my mood, but usually it was men's clothes, because I was really too ugly to be a girl even with my beard shaved, even though I did have breasts, and a cunt. Right under my cock. You can imagine, now, why I'm not on a Team. It's the unwritten rule: Superheros have to be hard-bodied and attractive, especially if they're not very... er... masculine. Or, if they're ugly, they have to be great mounds of solid muscle like Geist. Fat little hairy hermaphroditic mutants are just not going to make it. I mean, who wants that on a promotional poster? It won't sell jobs to the Team.

There's also the fact that my talents aren't much use for fighting anyway. It's a good thing that I found this job under Zephyrus's generosity, where I can live safely and hide from the world and sarcastically ride herd on the hard-bodied, attractive people in costumes. I'm not even very brave. Taking on an enemy infiltrator would be a ridiculous idea.

As I watched from around the corner, the intruder shifted and changed. She gained height, her skin darkened to *café au lait*, her hair shrank to dark and curly, and her outer skin took on the shape and sheen of a finely tailored men's suit. I hadn't seen her facial features well before, but as she turned in my direction I could see the face of Firecracker, our team's pyro. Proud, sleek, debonair, Lucius Dubarry not only gave the team class but a minority point as well. She'd even got the small diamond stud in his nose right. Perhaps she'd been studying him.

Then, as I stood there, she turned and saw me.

I should have forced a smile onto my face. I should have waved and hailed him, walked on by, then sounded the alarm. Instead, I froze. Her—Lucius's—face was impassive; I wondered for one moment what she could possibly be thinking, and then I knew that I had to be thinking of something myself, something smart, or she was going to Know and then I would Die. And, of course, the craziest thought in the world came into my head, and what else could I do? Maybe there was one part of my brain that was sick of my gorgeous coworkers and their clear contempt for me, the jokes about my anatomy that I almost didn't overhear. Maybe I wanted to get back at Firecracker for what he had that I never would. At any rate, what I did was to walk right up to that tall figure and say,

"You came back. I knew you would. I knew you couldn't resist." And then I put my hands on her shoulders and kissed those chocolate lips.

I felt her stiffen, almost flinch. There was a moment when I kissed a closed mouth, and then it opened and let me penetrate, a little. I can't imagine what must have been running through her head; Lucius was well known in his profile—and I'm sure that they all had the profiles of our Team, and even the staff, even my own, just as we had theirs—as an extremely heterosexual ladies' man. The idea that he'd let me kiss him was lunacy; if I hadn't been giving our intruder some tongue, I'd have been grinning from ear to ear. I backed off and whispered, "It's all right, Luke. You know you can trust me, like you always do. I never tell anyone about it, I never will. It's all on the down-low, like always." I paused, and then whispered, "But I knew you'd sneak back to see me."

She swallowed—I saw that one and bit my lip to keep from grinning—and then whispered back, "So... what is it that you want?" No name; I'm not that important and I expect that she didn't know me, was racking her brains as I'd racked mine. Ha. For the moment, I had the upper hand. Now, of course, I should make excuses and get away from this fictional tryst. Except that it seemed that the part of me who'd come up with this harebrained scheme was in control, not the sensible part that wanted, very much, to live.

"Whatever you're willing to give me. As always," I said, and I took that supervillain by the hand and led her toward my basement room.

I watched her scan the place as we entered, noting every wall and door, the bathroom off to the side. Of course; she'd assume that Firecracker would know it well. In actuality, Lucius had never been down here to this converted storage space with its secondhand furniture and sagging bed covered in books. I watched for a flash of contempt, but there was none, just... watchfulness. I saw Firecracker's visage reflected in the mirror as we passed, and my own. I looked away with a grimace. How did I get to be born this way? Damned if I know. My mother was a teenage junkie who gave her freakish half-goat baby up at birth, and when I hunted her up years later to find out my origins, she was already dead. The doctors told me that less than half of my hundred or so chromosomes were human, and the rest? Who knew? I did a lot of research once, on demons and satyrs and other creatures that I'm supposed to look like. They're all myths, you know. I never got any further than that. Never. So who cares? I'm just a mutant, like the scores of mutants wandering the underbellies of the cities, looking for work.

But now I had more crucial things to worry about, like the dark, deadly figure that had just settled carefully on the edge of my bed. After my earlier confidence, my acting that had seemingly convinced her, there was no way to back off now. My secret-paramour persona—yeah, right, me as anyone's secret paramour—needed to be solid, to never crack, even though I was shaking inside at the thought of what I was about to do.

So I started slow. Lucius and I were already lovers, I'd made that clear, but I'd also made it clear that he was a bit skittish about the whole thing, probably needed to be seduced anew each time even though he wanted it badly. I took her face gently in my hands and kissed Lucius's handsome features again—lips, brow, chin, ears, back to the lips again. This time, she let me have even more tongue. This time, she kissed me back. My cock flushed to hardness in an instant, and I could feel my cunt gushing and my nipples hardening against my old flannel shirt. I quickly opened a couple of buttons on my shirt and took her hand; moved it to my breast. My tits were bigger than hers, long and floppy, and hairy. *Yeah, feel that, baby. Guess you've never touched anything like that before, have you? But you can't do anything but pretend you want it, can you?* The thought turned me on. Apparently, so did the danger, because I was fast losing any fear at all to straight-up lust. Lucius's body was gorgeous, and I was happy to fuck it—there wasn't a member of that polished, dangerous, contemptuous Team that I hadn't used as jerkoff fodder—but it was the inhuman-looking woman inside that I really wanted.

Her fingers found my nipple. "Pinch it," I breathed in her ear. "Hard—you know how I like it." She didn't, but it didn't matter because I'd just told her, and I gasped and wriggled between her spread knees with the sensation. I cradled the back of her head and gave her tongue again while she worked my nipple, and then moved her other hand to my crotch. I always wear loose pants, and my hard-on was straining at the fabric. She did something deft and probably not quite human-fingered down there to get my belt and fly open. *Did you just shift a bit there, honey? Couldn't resist, couldn't do it the slow way, eh? Don't worry, I won't say a word.* Her hand curled around my cock and I moaned into her mouth.

Her grip slid all the way to its base, and then one fingertip caught the wetness oozing upward between the split testicles. She paused—*watch it, honey, you're supposed to know about that, and like it*—and then the finger found its way into my slit and worked its way up. *That's right, be bold. Lucius would be, or at least you think he would. Are you a straight girl? Probably. Except for Zephyrus, they're all straight, and even if they weren't they wouldn't want me.* My hand dipped experimentally into her lap, but she caught it and pulled her mouth away from mine. "I'll just dump these clothes," she said, getting up and moving towards the bathroom. Lucius's face smiled warily at me as the door closed.

Oh, that's right; those weren't real clothes, and she didn't want to have to peel them off in front of me. The feel of the "fabric" had been so convincing that I'd forgotten. She must have worked hard on that, over the years. I had a mental flash of her shaping her skin, again and again, comparing it to the fabric clothes spread out next to her, staring at the line of drape and crease. Was it exciting to her, the first time she went out naked and no one knew? I shucked my own clothes, hopped onto the bed, pushed off all the books onto the floor, and waited.

Lucius's form came out, all caramel muscles and white teeth and an enormous dark hard-on. *Bet you don't know what his dick really looks like, honey. Bet you're hoping against hope that you got it right.* Actually, I did know what it looked like, because I'd been in the shower room with him, and it was a lot smaller than mine. I grabbed mine and fingered it, looking her in the eye. "I know you want it, super-fucker," I said. "Come here and suck me off."

The white toothy smile wavered, but she gamely climbed onto the bed and lowered her mouth towards my dick. As warm wetness closed around it, I wondered briefly if she was planning to kill me during this bout of sex. After all, I had been stupid enough to bring her to this small basement room. It wouldn't be hard at all. I grabbed the dark head with its kinked hair and shoved it down over my cock. *If you're going to kill me, you're going to do it with my dick in your mouth, baby.* There was a grunt and a moment's resistance, and then just a warm wet sheath. *Well, of course she could reshape her throat. Probably doesn't even have a gag reflex unless she wants one.* What a way to die. I pumped my hips and fucked Lucius's face. This was pure fantasy; for a moment I let myself forget whose eyes lay behind that face. This was just me getting one over on one of those perfect people whose posters were plastered all over this building.

After a minute, I pulled the dark curly head up and shoved it down further, between what might have been overly large labia and might have been a split scrotum, but was actually a half-made melange of both. My cunt was dripping, and I shoved her face right into it. "Eat it, sweetheart," I breathed. "Lick it good. I know you want it. I know you want me." Pure porn, tacky as hell but I might as well indulge it. A wet tongue licked up and around my hole, then inside, then deeper ... *ohmigod, was that longer than human? Watch it honey, that's not one of Lucius's superpowers, not that I'm going to complain for so much as a second.* I was getting very close to going over the edge, so I let that tongue probe me for a moment and then I jerked her head back up, shoving my cock back into her mouth and coming.

I think that I bucked and shrieked for at least two minutes. When I come, I come hard. Not only did the figure whose head I had clamped to my groin not choke, but after it was over I discovered that I was still alive. "You are beautiful," I told her breathlessly, knowing that she'd think it was for Firecracker, but meaning it for her, herself. I leaned down and kissed her, tasting myself on her lips and tongue... I ran my tongue around hers, but it was safely normal-sized again. When I pulled back, Firecracker's face was grinning, and I had the distinct feeling that it wasn't an act. That made my stomach flutter, and for one second I felt suddenly shy. Then it occurred to me that she was probably thinking about how well she was fooling me. Oh well.

Since she hadn't killed me yet, I wasn't about to stop. "Come up here," I said, and she levered that long dark muscled body up onto the bed. A hard-on bobbed obligingly between her legs; I saw her surreptitiously glance at it, as if to make sure that she'd done it right, and bit back a smile. Quickly straddling her, I sank down onto it with a moan, my own semi-hard cock flopping against her tight belly. I looked pale and bloated and hairy next to Lucius's body, but I thrust that thought away and started humping. "Come on, honey, move that ass," I said, gasping with exertion. "Don't make me do all the work." My hooves dug into her thighs. I found her hands with mine and entwined my fingers, pressing downwards for leverage. She pushed upwards and held me upright easily. Damn, this bitch was strong. This was probably the point where the dick inside me would explode into a mass of razor-tipped tentacles and shred me from the inside out, but I didn't care.

She was breathing hard, too, and not acting. I know acting, having been with quite a few whores. Perhaps she felt that if she had to fuck some staff mutant to keep her cover, she might as well lay back and enjoy it. I hoped that was the case, anyway. I decided to up the stakes and paused, pulling up off her cock and reaching for my nightstand. A quick fumble among the debris came up with a bottle of lube, and I squeezed out a good batch and stuffed as much as I could up my ass. Then I sat back down, carefully, guiding that cock into my butt inch by inch. She was motionless, waiting for me; I wished that I could ask her to make the tip of it narrower, pointier, easier for entry. Damn, she could probably reinflate it once it was inside me, pump it up like a sex toy. The thought brought me to full hardness again in front, and I slid all the way down onto her pelvis.

I stopped thinking during the next few minutes of raw fucking. It didn't matter who I was, who she was, or what might happen next; it was just two bodies straining and bucking in rhythm until, like a miracle, she came. I know faked orgasms—I can smell them—and this was real. I came a few thrusts later, my ass clenching around a spasming cock and my own cock slapping hard against her belly. I squirted onto Lucius's broad flat muscular chest, scooped it up with my finger, and brought it to her lips. They opened and sucked my finger in, taking the offering.

Then, suddenly, she shifted. The cock shrank and pulled back out of my ass so quickly that I gasped. The face and body underneath me rippled and changed, mocha being replaced with mottled yellow and orange and red. The eyes... I hadn't seen her eyes before. Mottled copper as a serpent's hide, the pupils were a snake's slits, and there were no lashes or brows. She stretched her mouth sideways, showing off a set of sharp lizard-teeth... that still had my finger clamped in their vise.

She looked at me, expression unreadable, and I looked at her. This is it. I'm going to die now. There was no reason for her to show herself unless I wasn't ever going to be able to tell anyone about it. My second thought was, is she wondering why I'm not freaking out? Then I thought, screw it. I'm not going to die with a lie on my lips. Let there be truth between us, even if it's the last thing I say.

I took a deep breath. "Well, hello there, beautiful," I said. I meant it, too. She was bizarre, but strangely beautiful to me. And who was I to judge someone's looks? "I'm glad you decided to show yourself," I said. "Lucius isn't my lover. I saw you in the hall, and I knew this was the only chance I'd ever get. Thank you for some of the best sex I've had in my life."

This time it was her turn to freeze. I could see emotions flashing across her face, but I couldn't quite read them—confusion? Rage? It loosened her grip on my finger, though, and I quickly reclaimed it. Then she spoke—in her own voice, a rough contralto—and it was a string of blistering curses. Not specifically aimed at me, just curses. I captured her hands, lightly, not trying to restrain her. "It's all right," I said. "I won't tell anyone, and I'll help you get out of here. I can't help with whatever mission you were on, but at least I can make it a zero-sum. It's fair payment."

"I'm not a whore," she grated out, her nails digging into my hands.

"No," I said, "but you are one very fine lay. Even if you were just pretending to be interested in me. I hope it wasn't too... difficult. God knows that I'm not one of the better-looking mutants." I heard the curl of bitterness in my voice and shut my mouth. That wasn't supposed to come out. No use whining about spilled genetic material.

Her face stilled, eyes seeking out mine. I still couldn't read her, but I moved away respectfully as she sat up. Her skin was smooth, silken, almost artificial-feeling; I copped one last feel, caressing her thigh as I got off her. She looked at me and I removed my hand. "I'd rather have done it with you as you are," I said, "but playing with Lucius's body was fun too."

"So you were just toying with me the whole time," she said. There was danger in her tone, but I'd come too far to care.

"Not toying," I said. "I've never been more serious. I just wanted you. That's all. I didn't even think about anything else."

I didn't expect the look in her eyes. *Has no one ever wanted you for yourself? Not you, either?* It was only one second of naked feeling, but it took the rage out of the room and left it strangely empty, uncomfortable. "I'm sorry," I said.

The light in her eyes changed, became wilder. "You want me?" she hissed. "You think you want me?" Then the back of her hand latched onto my neck and she kissed me. This kiss was all scraping teeth, all bloated tongue that wormed its way impossibly long, chokingly long, into my mouth. I took it all, grabbing her back, digging my nails into her, wrapping my oddly-jointed furred bony legs around her. *Fuck yes.* I bore down, in a way that I hadn't done in years, and released a cloud of musk from scent glands that normal people didn't have. The smell rose, dizzying, heavy, surrounding us. Chimera might be able to alter a lot of bodily things, but she still had to breathe. Her lungs still carried molecules into her bloodstream, and she wouldn't be expecting this. It would drive her into a frenzy of half-dazed lust for at least a half hour, by which time... I'd have thought of something else, assuming that I still breathed myself.

Why hadn't I used that talent, that mutant power, on her before?

(Because people tended not to remember what they did under its drugging haze, and I *wanted* her to remember me.) Why didn't I go around using it on people right and left, making them fall helpless into my lecherous arms? Why wasn't I surrounded by throngs of dazed harem slaves? Why was I sleeping alone in the basement of a second-rate Team company, with no one knowing I had any powers at all? (I've got two, that I know of. We won't even discuss the second one.) That's what you're wondering, isn't it?

Well, maybe I'd just prefer people to want me for myself, you know? I'd tried the other way, plenty of times in my youth, and it never lasts. They wake up, they get disgusted, and they leave. After a while, it's not worth it unless you're desperately horny and can't take it any more. And it's kind of sleazy and embarrassing, you know? Not something to put on the resume. In fact, I hadn't told anyone about it in over a decade. And there's a reason why I'm working for a superhero team and not a supervillain team. I may not be brave, I may not be all that good, even, but I like to think I'm not a shit. That's where fragile self-esteem starts: At Least I'm Not An Asshole.

Now, however, there was a very good chance that I was fighting for my life, and all bets were off. The crazy suicidal urge that had put me here in the first place had evaporated with Lucius's imaginary features; this was real now, and I needed to even the playing field. I felt Chimera choke as she breathed in my musk, and shudder. She bit down, and I barely got my tongue out of the way in time. Instead, I bit down on the phallic tongue that was invading my throat. She hadn't choked me. I might not have her abilities at shapeshifting my orifices, but I am damn experienced at every kind of oral sex there is. It helps, when you look like me.

I pushed her backwards onto the bed and thrust my hand between her legs. Nothing. Smooth as a doll's crotch. Perhaps she didn't bother with genitals unless she was going to be using them. She bothered with small breasts and a female-looking form, though. Well, I was hardly one to complain to someone about their particular combination of primary and secondary sexual characteristics. "Give me a cunt," I said. "Now, or I'm going up your ass."

Her eyes were glazing over, but she heard me enough. The smooth flesh rippled under my touch, and blossomed outward. Labia opened like flower petals in fast-motion, and I found the hole between them. It was dry, so I scooped some extra lube out of the crack of my ass and went in. She growled and grabbed me by the hair; I shoved more of my hand into her. We were eye to eye. Even through the haze of my weapon, she was there, and I spoke to her. "Of course I want you," I said. "Of course I find you beautiful. I won't insult you by thinking that anyone else has ever found you anything but beautiful. Now open the fuck up." I shoved in further.

"Bastard," she whispered. "What if I grow teeth there and bite your hand off?" That almost made me pause, but I saw the corners of her mouth turn up. She was playing my game, then. *Fuck yes.*

"I know that you can kill me," I said. "But if you bite my hand off, this fuck will stop right now. And I don't think you want it to stop, or you'd have said something, right, honey?" I bore down and pressed out a bit more musk to back up my words. "Open up more. More. I know you can fucking do it, open up!" Her flesh yielded and my whole fist went in, up to the wrist. It would have to be my fist, because my cock had come twice and was out of commission for a while. "Give me that tongue again, baby," I said, and locked my mouth to hers again while my forearm did the pile-driver act. If the other orgasm had been real, this one was realer; she nearly broke my wrist with the whiplashing of her body. No human spine moved like that. No human cunt spat me out so deliberately, and sealed up behind me, either.

We both lay quietly for a while, pressed up against each other, probably both contemplating our next moves. It wasn't snuggling; I could feel tension in both our bodies. She was still foggy; I could see it in her eyes. "What have you done to me?" she asked. "And how long will it take to wear off, you fucker?"

I decided that honesty was still the best policy. Push a little, then pony up; push a little, then pony up. It was a dangerous game, indeed. "It's just something I can do," I said. "It'll wear off soon. Then I'll help you get out of here. Unless you think you can keep going." Then I rolled over onto my belly, bare-ass upwards, legs spread. It was a position of vulnerability, saying, *I trust you.* I wanted to see what she'd do.

What she did was to put an arm around me and pull me back onto my side, so that she was up against my back. She was still for a moment, breathing, and then the smooth groin against my buttocks shifted, and I felt something growing and prodding me from behind. *Fuck yes. I think I have you, girl. I'm not sure what I'm going to do with you, but I think I actually have you.* "Do you want me?" I whispered. That was an extra-dangerous question. It hung in the air between us, smelling like lifetimes of contemptuous glances, high-pitched uncomfortable laughter, people who pulled away from accidental contact with you on the subway. *How does it feel to never be wanted for who you really are?* I didn't know her history, I didn't know if she had other lovers, perhaps ones who were waiting at home for her right now and wondering what was keeping her. I doubted it, though. I had a feeling that her self-possessed coldness enclosed a loneliness just as deep and solitary as mine. While she was still half-hazy, I wanted to invoke that, to give a small haven to it ... something that could never be found elsewhere. *I'm not the enemy, honey. There's an enemy out there that's bigger than Teams and laws and governments, and we face that one on the same side. The rest, that's just what we do. This is who we are. Mutant. Outcast. I know, I know, I know.*

"Don't... put yourself down," she said. Her voice was suddenly soft, a timbre I'd never heard before. "You're not unworthy..." she fished for the words, "... of desire." *Oh, yes, you know, honey. You know what it feels like. I think I have you.*

I put my hand between my legs and took hold of the cock that was growing from her groin. This one wasn't even cock-shaped; I don't think she was even trying at that point. It was just tubular, bulging, throbbing against me. My ass was still lubed from earlier. "Do you want me?" I asked again. It wasn't the game any more. I just needed to hear it.

A pause, a few heavy breaths against my ear, then: "I want you." Her arm tightened around me. "I can't promise anything—"

"No promises after today," I said breathlessly. "This isn't about our loyalties. It's time out of time, space out of space. Nothing counts here except us. You want me? Take me." I moved the end of her appendage into the crack of my ass and felt it slowly slide in. We rocked there for a while, together; it wasn't the raw fucking of earlier, just locked-together comfort. Her breath slowly synchronized to mine. I relaxed, staring at her hand on my shoulder. It had no nails any more, just vague clubbed fingers, but it was all right, Actually, everything was all right.

Then one of the green lights on the panel on my wall lit up. "Shit," I said angrily, and she pulled away from me, and out of me. "Fucking hell."

"What's the matter?" she asked warily.

"Lupita's home." The monitor showed whose cars were in the parking garage; there was one in every staff bedroom. Zephyrus believed in knowing where his people were, although he wasn't up to chipping us all. "We have to get you out of here." I stood up, grabbing for my clothes.

"I can take on one of the other forms—" she began.

"Of the Team members? Won't work. Lupita can smell like a dog, and she's half crazy and none too bright. No, we have to think of something else." I threw on my pants and an old sweater, and shuffled through my small refrigerator. "Raw garlic—that'll put her off, as long as she doesn't actually see you."

"So why are you doing this?" Chimera asked casually. I could feel her closing back up, forcing the last of the drugging musk from her mind—that was good, she'd need all her wits to help me—becoming once again the supervillain who'd invaded Zephyrus's citadel. "Why don't you just turn me in?" *You haven't even asked why I'm here,* lay unsaid between us.

"Why didn't you kill me when you had the chance?" I asked, deliberately phrasing it that way. I was her way out now; I could say that.

She was silent for a moment. "I like you," she said. "You're... different." At my snort, she laughed—the first time I'd heard her laugh—and retorted, "No, really. I don't mean *that*. You wouldn't believe how some of the people on my Team look. You want disgusting?"

"Are they disgusting on the inside too?" I asked, popping raw garlic cloves into my mouth and trying not to gag as I crunched and swallowed.

"...Yes. Some of them. Some, not."

I opened a nip bottle of Jaegermeister and splashed it all over my sweater. That ought to distract Lupita. "Any of them your lover?"

She smiled wryly. "... No. Not now." *Ha. I knew it.* "What I mean is, you're not full of yourself. You're..."

"Real. In spite of the fact that I look like a mythical monster." I grabbed my big overcoat. "How small can you make yourself? Not tiny, flat."

"My basic internal organ space needs to stay the same mass," she said, "and I can't move it around too much. But once I fit down into a two-cubic-feet box."

"Right," I said. And so it was that I carried her to the parking garage under my overcoat. Her arms and legs were wrapped around me like flat bands; her grotesquely compressed head and torso pressed against my belly. To hide the lump, I carried two economy-size open bags of garlic-flavored potato chips, which also added to my scent. When I passed Lupita in the hall, she sniffed and curled her lip. I saluted her with a garlic chip and a drunken leer, and she kept walking.

Outside the perimeter of the robot-guards and out of sight of the cameras, I put down the chips and opened my coat. Chimera slithered out onto the broken asphalt lot, shook herself violently, and stood up. I looked up at her. She was almost a head taller than me. "Anything to say?" I asked. Stupid.

"No," she said, and turned, vanishing into the darkness.

"Right," I said after her. Then, reeking of booze and all, I walked to the all-night convenience store and bought yet more alcohol. This, I intended to actually get drunk on. The clerk gave me the hairy eyeball, but I didn't care. My give-a-damn switch had somehow gotten stuck off. Maybe she'd done it to me. Superfuckers.

∾

I wasn't usually a drunk, and the hangover I gave myself was bad enough that I spent the next day in bed. I should have said something to the Team about how their security had been breached— I could have made something up about seeing a shadowy figure—but I didn't. I stayed in bed and felt miserable, and slept off and on until noon the next day. I fended off the single knock with an excuse of illness, and pulled the covers over my head.

Finally, I went back to work. The newsletter still needed to get done, there was Manifesto's research notes to decipher and type, and Zephyrus wanted to add another page to the website. Weeks passed, and things fell back into their old routine. Then another staff member came through with the mail and handed me a birthday card from my Aunt Hazel. Except that I don't have an Aunt Hazel, and my birthday had gone by a month ago. My heart practically flung itself against my rib cage; I found that I was holding the letter as if it was a bomb that might go off at any moment.

Inside, a garish card wished me many happy returns, signed by Aunt Hazel. On the back, near the bottom corner, was a message in tiny writing. 2/8—10pm—McDonalds—1ˢᵗ St.

Shit.

∾

Of course I went. What, I was going to sit there at home and stare at the clock while my appointment went by? I buried myself in a burger and fries, deliberately not looking up at the passersby. It wasn't as if I could figure out which one she'd be, anyway. Ten o'-

clock went by, and then several excruciating minutes, and I was just about to get up and leave when someone slipped into the seat across from me.

It was a woman, looking like a fashion model with long red hair and a red leather coat. I was pretty sure the coat was real, not so sure about the miniskirt under it. "Hey," I said.

For one moment her eyes flashed, and the pupils shrank to slits. Then they were normal wide green eyes. "Hey," she said. Her lips were wide and red and perfectly formed.

Did you dress up for me, honey? Honesty, just enough of it to keep you interested. "I liked you better with your own face," I said.

She looked pissed at that. "I have to look like something!" she retorted. "Would you be seen on the street with me, wearing my own face?"

I looked her in the eye. "Yes," I said. *Try me.*

She shook her head. "You're crazy." To my surprise, there was admiration in her tone. "I notice you're not exactly out of the closet." She gestured at my covering clothing, my hat and boots.

I shrugged. "I'm only out here because you asked me. And I'm hoping that you're not going to ask me to be your spy, or contact, or anything like that. I'm hoping that you're here for you, and not for anyone else."

She looked as if she didn't know whether to be angry or flattered. I just looked at her. Finally, she dropped both of them. "I wasn't going to ask you that," she said. "I didn't think you'd be the type to go along with it, anyway."

"What, me all honorable and truth-justice-American-Way?" I snorted at that.

"No. I just figured you wouldn't be the type to let anyone get that kind of hold on you." Her green gaze was clear and straight, and a chill ran up my spine. *You read me.*

"Did you tell anyone about us?"

"No. You?"

"Obviously not. So why am I here?"

She reached across the table, tentatively. I supposed that my tone had been cranky, because she took my hand as if she expected it to be pulled away. "I... want to see you again." It sounded like it took quite an effort for her to say that.

"Consorting with the enemy? Why?" I wasn't going to make it easy. Not with the risk behind it. I had to be sure it was going to be worth it. Damn if I was going to let myself be desperate.

She looked down at her hand, resting on mine. I didn't move

it. "Time out of time," she said. "Space out of space. Away from all of them, just us." She looked up. "It's been a long time. I want more of that. I... want you." Her eyes were too proud to beg.

"I want you, too," I whispered. "Where? When?" *All right, there went my security, my safe little haven. Damn it.*

We ended up in the rest room—to this day I'm not sure whether it was the men's or women's room—fucking wildly with every kind of combination that you can do up against a tile wall while trying to be dead silent. The red leather coat, yes, that was real and discarded onto the floor. The rest dissolved into orange-red tie-dyed woman with blunt fingers and copper eyes. Didn't stay that way, at least not entirely, but that was all right too. *She'd be anyone for me, I realized, as long as she knows I want her best this way.* We left the McDonald's in normal drag, made it across the street, and didn't get any further than a dumpster in a deserted back alley, which gave us cover as we did it all over again on the slimy asphalt. This time she used her hands, and showed me what a shapeshifter's hands could do to someone, inside and out. Instead of screaming, I drew blood on her several times. The rents in her orange-red skin closed over almost immediately—not healed, as she explained to me later, just sealed up temporarily because she wasn't going to let a little bleeding stop us.

Later, we sat in the park together. Not on a bench—too obvious. In the bushes. Neither her place nor my place was safe, and we weren't up to the risk of a motel room just yet, even in a different city. "Yeah," I said. I knew we were supposed to be talking, certainly there was serious stuff to say, but I couldn't think of anything.

"Yeah," she said. There was silence for a few more minutes, then: "Do you ever just want to throw it all over, go live somewhere no one's trying to fight over the scraps, no one's trying to push some mission on the world? Just have a life?"

"Yeah," I said. "All the time." There, she'd gone and done it; voiced something I wasn't ready for. Not now, anyway. But there might come a time... My hand slipped into hers, carefully. Tentatively. She allowed it.

"When I have sex," she started, almost haltingly, "I'm different people for different people. But I'm always normal, always pretty. Never..."

"Yourself?" I asked. "Somehow I can't see someone like you craving normality. Not in bed, anyway."

She laughed at that. "In bed, no. Nor even in the rest of life. I'm just tired of being what people want me to be. Sometimes I've done things in bed just to freak them out, just to watch them run, when I can't take it any more. But you... don't run away."

"Nope. If I want someone, I want them the way they are." *Like I want them to want me. But I have no pretty face to put on. Perhaps that's a blessing, in its own way.* Her hand squeezed mine at that. *We understand each other.*

"Next week?" she asked. "Same time and place?" Her hand took on a sudden obscene shape, flirtatiously throbbing against my palm.

"Different one," I said. "Send me another card from Aunt Hazel."

"Right," she said, lifting her obscene fingers to my lips. I kissed them, then did more than kiss. Then she sighed and pulled away, and was gone.

"Right," I said to the empty air, brushing the pine needles off of me. The problem with being furred is that leaves and pine needles are always sticking to you. Rolling in the bushes becomes a serious grooming issue, every time. Next time I'd ask her to pick me clean. I'm sure that those fingers could become tweezers, in a pinch.

Next week, the card came, with a longer note on the back. Behind the Burger King. Eleven o'clock. Bring a garbage bag, lotion, and some steel wire. There's this fantasy, you see... no one else would understand.

Fuck yes.

About the Author

Raven Kaldera is the author of 34 books and innumerable short stories. He lives on a small homestead in Massachusetts with his polymorphously perverse polyamorous family, and a few goats, sheep, and chickens. 'Tis an ill wind that blows no minds.

Scheherazade's Façade, ed. Michael M. Jones
The gender lines are blurred and transcended in twelve tales of magic, self-discovery, and adventure, penned by some of today's most intriguing authors. In these pages, you'll find heroes and villains, warriors and tricksters, drag queens and cross-dressers, tragedy and triumph. Featuring all-new work from Tanith Lee, Sarah Rees Brennan, Alma Alexander, Aliette de Bodard, and more, Scheherazade's Façade is filled with surprises and beauty, and may just challenge the way you see the world.

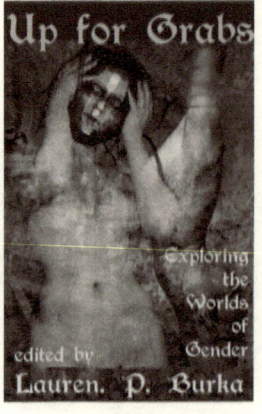

Up For Grabs: Exploring the Worlds of Gender
ed. Lauren P. Burka
An anthology of erotic stories where gender is up for grabs. Thousands of people spend time on the Internet identified with a gender other than the one they were born with, for erotic gratification or to stretch their imaginations. But what if you got a tax break for changing your gender? What if you could choose to be no gender at all until you went on a date?

Up For Grabs 2: Exploring More Worlds of Gender
ed. Lauren P. Burka
As editor Lauren P. Burka says in her introduction, "All erotica is the story of sex breaking free from biological need to become the co-conspirator of pleasure." Never is that more apparent than in the sharp-eyed, sharp-minded stories she has selected here by asking the question "What happens to sex if we let go of every assumption we have about gender and start from scratch?"